CONVALESCENT CONVERSATIONS

BY

LAURA RIDING

Convalescent Conversations
by Laura Riding
{Laura (Riding) Jackson}

© George Fragopoulos and Ugly Duckling Presse, 2018
© Cornell University Library, 2018
Introduction © Mark Jacobs & George Fragopoulos, 2018

Originally published in 1936 by
The Seizin Press (Deya, Mallorca) and Constable & Co (London)

Published with the permission of Cornell Universty Library
and the Estate of Laura (Riding) Jackson

First Edition, First Printing, 2018
ISBN 978-1-937027-85-8

Ugly Duckling Presse
The Old American Can Factory
232 Third Street #E303, Brooklyn, NY 11215
www.uglyducklingpresse.org

Lost Literature Series #20

Distributed by SPD/Small Press Distribution (USA);
Inpress Books (UK); Raincoast Books via Coach House Press (Canada)

The publisher acknowledges the generous support of
the National Endowment for the Arts
and the New York State Council on the Arts.

Cover design and typesetting by Don't Look Now!
The type is Caslon and Futura

Printed in the USA by McNaughton & Gunn
Bound by McNaughton & Gunn
Covers printed letterpress at Ugly Duckling Presse
Cover paper provided by Materials for the Arts

CONVALESCENT CONVERSATIONS

BY

MADELEINE VARA
(LAURA RIDING)

WITH AN INTRODUCTION
BY GEORGE FRAGOPOULOS

Lost Literature Series No. 20
Ugly Duckling Presse, Brooklyn, NY

INTRODUCTION

VIRGINIA WOOLF BEGINS her 1930 essay "On Being Ill" with the following observation:

> Considering how common illness is, how tremendous the spiritual change that it brings, how astonishing, when the lights of health go down, the undiscovered countries that are then disclosed…when we think of this, as we are so frequently forced to think of it, it becomes strange indeed that illness has not taken its place with love and battle and jealousy among the prime themes of literature.[1]

"Novels, one would have thought," Woolf continues, "would have been devoted to influenza; epic poems to typhoid; odes to pneumonia; lyrics to toothache."[2] *Convalescent Conversations* can, in part, be read as Laura Riding's answer to Woolf's implicit challenge to create a literature that represents illness as part of the human

---

1 Virginia Woolf. "On Being Ill." *The Collected Essays, Vol. 4.* (New York: Harcourt, Brace and World, 1967), 193.

2 Ibid.

experience—although illness, in this particular novel, also serves as a metaphor for broader philosophical and political stakes that surpass the solipsistic confines of a single body. But unlike Woolf, whose aesthetic call is driven by realist tenets, Riding's novel is an attempt to break away from the realist tradition that pervades much of modernist literature.

Convalescent Conversations was published in 1936 under Riding's pseudonym, Madeleine Vara, by Seizin Press, which she ran with Robert Graves, who was at the time both lover and collaborator; this was the same year in which Riding and Graves would flee Mallorca and Franco's fascism. The novel tells the story of Adam and Eleanor, two convalescents in an unnamed sanitarium who begin a peculiar courtship. Thomas Mann's *The Magic Mountain*, first published in 1924, looms as an important precursor, at least in regards to the novel's themes. And much like Mann's novel, the backdrop of the sanitarium and the pervading sense of illness and decrepitude, both physical and spiritual, allow Riding to develop her own satirical take on the experience of living in modernity.

Following the dramatic form of Riding's earlier *roman à clef 14A*, which she co-wrote with George Ellidge and published in 1934, most of *Convalescent Conversations* takes place in dialogue: the developing relationship between Adam and Eleanor is presented in a series of philosophical discussions on topics including religion, the meaning of God, the nature of language, and relations between men and women. There is no real plot to speak of, and even less action. The claustrophobia that Adam and Eleanor feel is often felt by the reader, too. At certain moments, Riding's protagonists seem like precursors to Samuel Beckett's clowns, existential figures confronting the absurd nature of existence itself. (Eleanor: "Everyone is really everyone else. And the answer is nobody.") We are never told what it is that Adam and Eleanor suffer from, a fact that further opens their illnesses to interpretation as metaphor—the rise of fascism in Europe being the most obvious, though certainly not the only, shadow narrative a reader might consider. Furthermore, and thinking beyond the thematic concerns that the novel presents its readers with, the experimental form of *Convalescent Conversations* allows Riding to examine the generic limitations of the modernist novel itself.

In her autobiography, *The Person I Am*, Riding writes of her disdain for what she views as the "impatience" of the modern world toward "the problem of human self-knowledge."[3] This impatience, "peculiar to this century's intellectual modernism," has "developed into a cynicism of mistrust"[4] in regards to how the realities of of modern existence have been represented in literature, philosophy and the arts. For Riding, the

---

3 Laura (Riding) Jackson. *The Person I Am, Vol. 1*, eds. John Nolan and Carol Ann Friedman (Nottingham: Trent Editions, 2011), 38.

4 Ibid.

realist novel is a symptom of this cynicism, part of what she calls an obsession with "modern psychological realism."[5] Riding views the actuality of the human, and of human experience, as ultimately resistant to literary representation, especially in the reified forms of realist fiction. This mistrust of modern psychology is also expressed through the novel's less than subtle attacks on Freudian psychology. In addition to dismissive allusions to the talking cure (Eleanor's last words are "Don't talk so much"), *Convalescent Conversations* subverts the conventions of psychological realism through its extensive, almost exclusive use of dialogue, which allows Riding to avoid representing the psychological inner workings of her protagonists' minds, a formal rejection of the kind of interiority championed by writers such as Woolf, James Joyce, and Marcel Proust.

Riding may be best known for a certain hermetic quality that renders, or attempts to render, her texts impervious to critical dissection; *Convalescent Conversations* is no exception to this aesthetic stance. For Riding, the trouble with critical discourse is that it often seeks to supplant the primacy of the text itself, transforming the literary object into something other than what it is. The irony of Riding's skepticism about literary criticism should not escape us: Riding and Graves' co-authored texts, *A Pamphlet Against Anthologies* and *A Survey*

---

5 Ibid.

of Modernist Poetry helped launch, if unintentionally, the New Criticism, one of the most influential schools of literary criticism of their century. Even if much later in life Riding would renounce much of her earlier work, both creative and otherwise, what remains, when all is said and done, is the work itself. May this return of *Convalescent Conversations* to print make the entirety of Riding's vision a little easier to glimpse.

— GEORGE FRAGOPOULOS

NOTE:

After marrying writer Schuyler B. Jackson in 1941, Riding officially changed her name to Laura (Riding) Jackson. We have decided to refer to the author as Riding and not (Riding) Jackson in this edition for two reasons: first, to maintain fidelity to the text as it was originally published; secondly, to emphasize the radical break between the Riding of the 1930s and the (Riding) Jackson who renounced most of her earlier work.

In almost all instances, this new edition replicates Riding's idiosyncratic style when it comes to typography, spelling, and punctuation. In only a few cases has the original text been modified, either to maintain consistency throughout the work or where the original seemed to contain an error.

ONE

Davis wheeled Eleanor far out on the veranda, to the left. Then she went in for Adam, wheeling him also far out on the veranda, but to the right.

'Is that Adam?' called Eleanor to Davis.

'I'll have a look,' said Davis, bending forward to study Adam's face. 'Is that you, Seventeen? The lady in Five would like to know.'

'Come, Davis,' said Adam, 'roll the lady along so she can see for herself.'

'It's not proper to roll ladies along to gentlemen.'

'Then roll gentlemen along to ladies.'

'That would also be against the laws of nature and courtship. Things must just seem to happen accidentally.'

'Well, could you just make it seem to happen accidentally,' said Eleanor, 'leaving out the courtship?'

Davis wheeled Adam a little toward Eleanor. 'You wouldn't deprive us poor nurses of a little romance, now would you, Miss Five?'

'You wouldn't deprive us poor convalescents of the little sympathy we can give one another, now would you, Davis?' Davis wheeled Eleanor within decorous talking reach of Adam's chair.

'Such as complaining to each other about the way us poor nurses abuse you poor convalescents.'

'Only one poor nurse and two poor convalescents,' said Adam.

'And what about poor Trebble?' asked Davis. 'Doesn't she count?'

'Oh, she only has to stay awake while we sleep, and think her own thoughts—and read *our* books,' said Eleanor.

'Well, it's no fun reading *your* books, Miss Five. "God help the nurse with an intellectual patient," I always say. But there really ought to be a rule against patients having poetry books.'

'Trebble can't accuse me of poetry books,' Adam said. 'And she has a perfectly good crime story this week.'

'Crime story,' snorted Davis, 'and poor Trebble just coming off an attempted suicide case.'

'But that ended happily,' Eleanor said. 'Crime stories don't end happily.'

'Don't they, now? It's crime stories that have all the happy endings these days, and love stories all the tearful ones. I don't know what's come over the world all of a sudden.'

At this moment Miss Kenwood, the matron, made a stately appearance on the veranda. Davis immediately thought of tucking in their rugs more securely.

'And how are our two healthiest patients this morning?' asked Miss Kenwood, bending her head toward them but not her body.

'You're not reproaching us, Miss Kenwood, are you?' Adam answered. As a matter of fact, she was, rather. But equally she seemed to reproach the patients who were not her healthiest. It was Miss Kenwood's faintly reproachful manner that kept patients of all degrees of illness from feeling themselves too much at home here. Miss Kenwood, for example, did not like patients suffering from nervous breakdowns. They always came prepared to stay; she liked patients to come prepared to go. Perhaps she was not the ideal nursing-home matron, but she certainly kept things moving. She regarded the nursing-home as a clearing-house; and her ambition for it and herself was probably that now and again it should be quite empty. Thousands of postmasters all over the world must have the same sort of impossible ambition: all the out-going letters in their sacks at the railway station, the collection-boxes empty, and the incoming letters not yet written, even.

Miss Kenwood, it was said, had been in Variety earlier in life. But now she wore a stiff black silk dress and a white lace collar, and was respectably stout. She gave the impression of knowing a great deal about life, and also of decently suppressing all she knew. One also felt that she knew a lot of jokes which she would never, never, tell again. All of which helped to prevent patients from feeling too much at home. The nurses might be ever so punctilious and condescendingly jolly, and the doctors ever so interested in their cases, but Miss Kenwood ruled the course of time; and Miss Kenwood, it had to be remembered, was not really interested. From the moment one entered the nursing-home one was made to feel that one must get it all over—dying or the recovering—as soon as possible.

Eleanor and Adam, being both brutally indifferent to their fate (and all the more so now that they were both out of danger), entirely agreed with Miss Kenwood. Eleanor had now for four days been well enough to be wheeled on to the veranda every morning, Adam for three. It might have been, as far as they were concerned, the veranda of an hotel at which they were stopping the night; the nursing-home might have been an hotel. They each lacked that morbid reverence for their illness which transforms nursing-homes, for most invalids, into temples of sacred memory, every detail of which must be engrained in their minds in tender invalid colours. Most invalids, that is, however aristocratic in their healthy life, have a tendency to vulgar emotional inertia in nursing-homes. But not so with Eleanor and Adam: they thoroughly understood Miss Kenwood's point of view. Perhaps it was Miss Kenwood's experience in Variety that made her so sensitive to the vulgarities of the aristocratic in their weak moments. She was now, so to speak, retired; and naturally she would be rather bored with vulgarity.

This sense of community with Miss Kenwood made them hope she would, perhaps, tell them just one joke before they left. They had discussed this on their first morning on the veranda together. On the second they had discussed themselves: Eleanor and Adam, until they met on the veranda, had only known each other through their nurses. First they had had the same night-nurse. Then they shared both night-nurse and day-nurse. This arrangement had been suggested by Miss Kenwood because there was a shortage of nurses, and because, though both had been ill enough, they seemed, of all her patients, the must brutally indifferent to their fate. People who are not so constituted are inclined, when ill, to attach great importance to the absoluteness with which they can say 'my nurse.'

How did it happen that Eleanor and Adam were both so brutally indifferent to their fate? Were they, then, so very old, or so very young, or so poor or so rich or so stupid or so intelligent, that nothing that happened mattered to them this way or that? No. They were of an average age (thirtyish) and average wealth and average intelligence—and average appearance, too. And it is only people like that who can afford not to care about themselves. For no matter what happens to them, no matter what they do, it is bound to be average all right—because they are like that. You may say off-hand that, why, most people are average. But if you think a little about all the people you know you will have to admit to yourself that there is something peculiar about every one of them. You hear a great deal about 'ordinary people' and the 'plain man'; and people are always saying querulously, 'I'm just a plain ordinary person like everyone else.' What they mean, of course, is that they are stupid and so is everyone else; and, of course, this is untrue. They are, rather than stupid, peculiar, obstinate and discontented. Very few people are really stupid, as very few are superlatively intelligent. And only one in a million has a really average intelligence: only one in a million is really serene. Practically everyone is more or less intelligent than everyone else; and the less intelligent ones are querulous, and the more intelligent ones are similarly excitable, each in his own way—one is 'sensitive', another 'intense', etc. But, as I have said, only one in a million is really serene, has that delicate evenness of mind that makes it possible not to complain, not to get excited, not to care—and yet to be trivially and comprehensively interested in everything that happens. Eleanor and Adam were, then, two in two million. It was a remarkable coincidence, I mean, that two people of such average intelligence should have met at all—one out of one million, the other out of another.

Their first morning together had been spent in discussing the nursing-home, the nurses and Miss Kenwood. They did not discuss the other patients; first, because they had not met them, and then because they knew them so well from what their nurses said about them. There was a maternity case, and such an adorable baby, though the mother was well over forty. It was her first, and she planned to have three more. Well, that was her business.

Then there was Lady Mary, whom so many well-known people came to see. That was rather dull; there was no suggestion, for example, that the Queen might possibly come to see her. And then Dr. Stanley Brown, who had had the usual old-man's operation. And Trebble's attempted suicide case: there were two men in it, and both had come to see the patient, and she had seemed quite happy, with everything starting all over again. And so on. One had Miss Kenwood's point of view there: one couldn't be bothered, beyond certain practical enquiries.

Then the nurses. Davis was young, handsome, efficient, and witty enough in a lazy Welsh way. Trebble was older, not every good-looking, suspicious of your feelings about her, no less efficient than Davis but a little tired-looking and melancholy, so that you felt rather apologetic that she had to do so many things for you: she did not, they agreed, make a very good nurse, exactly because you kept saying to yourself how kind she was.

Then Miss Kenwood. They both liked her, decidedly. They both had the feeling that she was full of jokes that she would probably never, never, tell you. They did not feel that she was one of their sort; people of average intelligence cannot, in fact, consider themselves to be people of a particular sort. They felt that she was just right for her job. She was one of those superfluous people who wisely reconcile themselves to the superfluous job. The nursing-home could have got on very well without her, but there she was; and no one resented her being there. Miss Kenwood lacked grace, good humour, sympathy, tact. But she had dignity. In Variety, and in telling jokes, and in fulfilling the superfluous job, dignity was the most important thing. It had nothing to do with intelligence. For example, some people, no matter how intelligent, were out of things; and if you were out of things it did no good to think about them, and no good to pretend to be stupid, either—that was just inviting other people to be rude to you. There were only two courses open if you were out of things and intelligent: to go mad or be dignified. Miss Kenwood was not the type to go mad.

TWO

O N THEIR SECOND MORNING together Eleanor and Adam talked about themselves. First they discussed childhood—because Adam had said that being ill was like being a child again; it was awkward being a child, and awkward being ill. Also, people behaved the same way to you. Eleanor would not agree that being ill was like being a child again. She had not enjoyed being a child, and she had enjoyed being ill. When you were a child people were always expecting things of you, and whatever you did was watched and weighed and commented on. When you were ill you were left pretty much to yourself. People were cruel to children, but kind to invalids. She remembered how she had dreaded her mother's talks with her. Her mother at that time used to write articles on children, using her as material. Her father at that time owned a fashionable shop where sporting accessories were sold. He regarded her, she knew, as something out of his line—just as if, for some reason, he had had to install a china department in his shop: he would have to be interested in it in a business way, but he'd never get really used to the idea. Then her mother and father had separated and she had been sent to live in the North with a sister of her mother's she had never seen; she supposed that her mother had by this time stopped writing articles about children and had no more need of her. She had been to school off and on, but she honestly couldn't remember what it had all been like. Everything had been so strange; the way one feels about foreign girls in foreign schools—that was how she had felt about herself. Then her mother had died and left her a good deal of money. She came to London, and took up this and that, but had never been able to get really absorbed in anything. There were so many people absorbed in so many things, and there didn't seem enough things to go round. It didn't seem fair to compete, since she had all the money she needed and wanted very little in the way of 'life' to make her comfortable.

She liked, best of all, talk. And most people were ready to talk. It was almost impossible not to have friends if you liked talk. What was a friend but someone who was willing to spend some of his free time with you in talk? Adam said that he, too, liked talk. Perhaps it was only a habit, because he had come of a large family. He had five sisters and one brother. He was the youngest, born of his father's second marriage. His brother, of the first marriage, was the oldest—old enough to be his father. His sisters, all also of the first marriage, were pretty old, too. Every one had been rather nice to him. His mother had been his father's housekeeper before he married her, and his half-brother and half-sisters had treated him like the housekeeper's child—distantly but not unkindly. He had

had, he was glad to say, a lower-class education: been apprenticed to a house-builder, and now he was an architect on his own. Architecture, he said, was a perfect job—an in-between work, neither a profession nor a business; just helpful, and it didn't kill you, and you never got too important. He couldn't see the sense of calling doctoring a profession. In the old days it had been openly recognized that doctoring was dirty work like any other lower-class job. Now everything was done to disguise this fact—top hats and gold watches; doctors went about mysteriously disguised as statesmen or successful authors.

On their third morning together Davis, as we know, teased them by wheeling them to opposite corners of the veranda. Then she wheeled them toward each other, and then Miss Kenwood appeared, and then Davis, having tucked them in and waited a moment (looking coolly down into the street) in case Miss Kenwood wanted anything of her, left the veranda without a word to anyone. Davis was one of those people who, though not what you would call polite, have good manners just because they fulfill subordinate positions with the right amount of independence; they don't ask you to be always considering their feelings.

In answer to Miss Kenwood's question, 'And how are our two healthiest patients this morning?' Adam had said, 'You're not reproaching us, Miss Kenwood, are you?' To this Miss Kenwood replied: 'Not exactly, but you mustn't think you can stay here for ever. In fact, I give you about a week, and no more.'

'But we haven't begun to walk yet,' protested Adam.

'Miss Kenwood will probably send us home in our chairs,' Eleanor said. 'Just roll us out into the street.'

'I couldn't possibly spare the chairs,' said Miss Kenwood.

'Oh, all right,' said Adam. 'We'll crawl home.'

Miss Kenwood almost smiled. She was going to tell them a story—a very short one.

'Once we had a young woman here suffering from a peculiar hysterical affection of the nerves: travelling paralysis, the doctors called it. Sometimes she couldn't talk, sometimes she couldn't move one leg or the other or both, or it might be her arms, or the whole left side or right side. And then some days she'd be quite all right, and we'd let her get up, and she'd seem so happy, thinking that she would be able to go on with her work now—she was studying dramatic art. And then all of a sudden it would come on her again. Well, it went on for nearly a fortnight like that, and then one day I had a visit from the Director of the dramatic-art school. Curiously enough, we had known each other in our younger days. At one time in my life I was also interested in dramatic art.' Here Miss Kenwood almost smiled again.

'The Director had an awkward tale to tell. She had heard some gossip at the school about this young woman's illness, and had finally got two of the students to confess. The travelling paralysis was the result of a wager. The young woman had been saying that a good actress could act convincingly in ordinary life as well as on the stage. But the end of it all was even stranger than the beginning. When we told her that we had found her out, she admitted the hoax but insisted that she really couldn't move her legs now. Of course we made her get up. And I must say that she didn't seem able to. What made me think of her was your talking about crawling home. She's the only patient who ever *crawled* out of here. And I don't think she was pretending.'

While telling this story Miss Kenwood had kept rhythmically bending her head (but not her body), now toward Eleanor, now toward Adam, and slowly folding and unfolding her hands, now in one direction, now in another. Eleanor and Adam did not say anything immediately. It was not a story to comment on or laugh at; it was not one of the jokes they suspected Miss Kenwood of being so full of. It was a cruel story. And yet they could feel no sympathy with the young woman, nor blame Miss Kenwood in any way. Why had she bothered to tell them the story at all? Eleanor thought she knew why. Miss Kenwood realized that she and Adam liked her, and this was her way of telling them that she liked them, without being too demonstrative: by trusting them not to think her cruel.

'I suppose a lot of people go through life,' Adam said, 'not even knowing that all the time they're only pretending.'

'If it makes them happier, why shouldn't they?' asked Eleanor.

'People never do things merely for the sake of being happy,' said Miss Kenwood. 'There's always something more behind it.'

'You're very cynical, aren't you, Miss Kenwood?' Adam said.

'No, I don't think so, but I've seen a lot of different kinds of people in my day. One can't help seeing. And I've never had the time to take people at their own valuation. *Nor* have I the time to stand talking philosophy with patients. Patients are always so fond of philosophy. Remember! In a week, out you go, both of you.' Miss Kenwood made a stately disappearance.

'She's a dear, isn't she?' said Adam.

'Not exactly,' Eleanor said, 'but she knows her humanity.'

'Do you believe that one learns things through "seeing," as she calls it? I've always felt that you either understand life or you don't. Question of grey matter.' He tapped his head.

'You might just as well say that you're either alive or not alive. Everyone understands *something*—or he's not alive. Even animals, and fish. Everyone understands at least one thing. The rest is a matter of application. Fish don't understand anything besides water because they're lazy. They're so lazy they don't even bother to understand themselves. Then, as life gets more energetic, interests multiply. There's more experience, more things to understand—so they get understood. Bigger brains, I admit, but not necessarily better ones. Take a cat: it knows what it knows at least as well as we know what we know.'

'What about birds?' asked Adam. 'All that nest-building and sense of direction? Is that as wonderful as they make out, do you think?'

'In my opinion, far less wonderful than frogs and toads and snakes—or even fish. The only really individual thing birds do is fly. As for nest-building, they have to live *somewhere*; and as for singing, that's all calling to mates in the most simpering way, every vote a soprano, and no real love of music, which is the only excuse if people *must* sing. And as for flying, it always strikes me as pretty idiotic. Where's the use in getting to places quick and rushing about from one place to another? That's why aeroplanes leave me cold, quite apart from the monstrousness of severing connexion with the earth, if only for a few hours. People talk of the wonders of communication and travel in modern life. But I call it deconcentration. All this air-mindedness—it's just bird-wittedness.'

'You certainly have very definite opinions about things,' said Adam. 'Not that I let myself get taken in by the works of man or the wonders of nature. For instance, every year you hear about people seeing the Green Ray at sunset, and the ecstatic sensation it gives them. Well, why shouldn't there be green rays—or blue rays or pink rays? Just think of the dark: is it any less strange that every day there comes a time when it gets dark?'

'And that every night there comes a time when it gets light?' said Eleanor.

'Yes, that's another joke. But does anyone laugh? And what is there that happens that isn't rather peculiar? What is a Green Ray that it should get any preference? To my mind it's all equally peculiar.'

'Oh, come now,' said Eleanor. 'Being ill is more peculiar than being well, surely?'

'Indeed not,' said Adam, stubbornly. 'Would you say that being dead is more peculiar than being alive.'

'And isn't it?' asked Eleanor. 'Lying stiff and still like that and being absolutely nobody?'

'And what about all the peculiar things you do when you're alive and somebody? Eating and drinking and getting cold and then hot and then sweating and then getting ill?'

'Aren't you contradicting yourself?'

'Of course I am. That's one of the peculiar things we don't do when we're dead.'

'No, only when we're ill.'

'Don't be silly.'

'You don't really think we're being anything but silly, do you?' asked Eleanor.

'I think we've been as serious as two philosophers. Didn't Miss Kenwood say patients were fond of philosophy?'

'You don't really think that philosophers are serious,

do you?' asked Eleanor.

'I'd like to know what else they are if they're not serious. Why, it's the only excuse they have. Take that away, and—'

'Take that away, and they're just talking. Like you and me. What better excuse can you ask?'

'But there has to be an excuse for talking,' Adam said. 'For instance, us. The demands of common politeness.'

Eleanor seemed to regard this as an excuse for silence: was he, after all, just tiresome? It was difficult to tell with men. They weren't naturally good talkers.

'I don't want to break in on any private reveries,' said Davis, coming up later, 'but it's time to go back to bed. It'll taste all the sweeter when you pick up the lost threads to-morrow.'

'Aren't you slightly mixing the metaphors?' asked Adam.

'I never was much good at keeping them separate,' said Davis.

THREE

On their fourth morning together Eleanor and Adam said very little to each other for the first ten minutes. They were able to sit up much straighter now, and so they naturally paid more attention to what was happening in the street below. The houses opposite the nursing-home had been converted into flats; there was an interesting variety, therefore, in the tenants. And on either corner was a shop—one a greengrocer's, the other a post-office and stationer's. The chief subject of interest in the street was a little girl, about three, in the charge of a very old man. She had pale fair hair, and thin legs, and wore a bright red coat. The very old man had a very crooked back; he would follow the little girl about, as she walked up and down with her doll's pram, and then suddenly leave her to go down into the basement. Perhaps he had something on the fire to watch. Perhaps he did all the housekeeping; for once he came up with the dustbin, and another time they saw him shaking a sheet out of one of the windows on the ground floor. Then the little girl's mother came out—out of the proper entrance. She was stout, and had bright fair hair, and wore very nice clothes. She bent down to the little girl, and the old man stood near, his hand to his ear to catch what was said. Then she went off, and soon the little girl was sitting on the house steps, the doll's pram in front of her. Another woman came out of the house, obviously from an upper flat, with a dog on a lead. She was slender, grey-haired and more elegant-looking than the little girl's mother, though her clothes were not so nice. She seemed annoyed to find the little girl in her way, and still more annoyed when her dog stopped to sniff at the doll's pram. The old man opened the gate for her, not in a servile way, but because he happened to be standing there. She did not thank him—or, at least, Eleanor and Adam did not see her lips move.

ELEANOR: Do you think that old man's any relation to the little girl?

ADAM: I think he must be, or the mother wouldn't trust her to him like that.

ELEANOR: *I* think he's the mother's father!

ADAM: Do you think she'd treat her father like that?

ELEANOR: You didn't see her treat him badly, did you?

ADAM: No, but he might be just a servant for all the notice she took of him.

ELEANOR: Old people like being useful. I think it's a very good idea, instead of having some fresh young girl waste her morning. There was a story in the newspaper about a woman of fifty who'd been a typist and couldn't get a job. So she killed herself, leaving a note saying that if she wasn't wanted at fifty, what would it be like when she was older? Now, it may be that a woman of fifty doesn't make such an efficient typist as a woman of twenty-five. But there must be a lot of doddering jobs-around-the-house that old people would be good for.

ADAM: That wouldn't leave much dignity to old age, would it?

ELEANOR: The so-called dignity of old age is based on respect for what people have done—not on respect for senility. I bet the mother of that little girl would treat the old fellow—supposing that he really is her father—a lot worse if he didn't make himself useful. She doesn't look too kind. Think what his life would be if he just hung about, grunting and wheezing and demanding respect.

ADAM: How do you know he doesn't grunt and wheeze all the same?

ELEANOR: People don't grunt and wheeze so much if they're occupied.

ADAM: But seriously, there aren't many old people with strength enough to do even light jobs.

ELEANOR: It's not a question of strength but of having time. Old people have more time on their hands than any other kind of people. First of all, they sleep less than other people. Get up early and prowl round the house. Well, why shouldn't they—very slowly—start getting breakfast?

ADAM: I'm glad I'm not *your* grandfather. When I'm an old man, I don't want to do anything but have privileges. I want to sit in a big chair by the fire and say exactly what I please, with no one daring to contradict me.

ELEANOR: Then I'm glad I'm not your granddaughter.

ADAM: There ought to come a time in everybody's life when what he says goes. All our lives, whatever we say is either dismissed or contradicted. When we're children no one takes what we say seriously. People listen and think, 'That child is going to grow up intelligent.' But when we've grown up intelligent, what happens? The more intelligent we are, the more they argue with us.

ELEANOR: If they don't argue with you when you're old it'll only be because they think you a doddering old fool.

ADAM: All right, then I'll be a doddering old fool. But at least I'll have the satisfaction of making them listen without interrupting—of hearing myself talk.

ELEANOR: Oh, if that's all your after . . . . I suppose, then, that now, for instance, in talking to you, I'm just interrupting—

ADAM: You needn't take me so literally. What I mean is that, until a person's old, even in mere talking it's constant warfare or submitting to all kinds of insults, in order to get a modicum of attention for your point of view or, it might be, your life's work.

ELEANOR: I hate that word 'modicum.'

ADAM: Well, what other word would you have me use?

ELEANOR: Wouldn't 'a little attention' do just as well?

ADAM: Perhaps it would. I'm not so sure. What's wrong with 'modicum,' anyway?

ELEANOR: Oh, it sounds so Latinistic, and it's not good Latin, only very dull English. And then people pretend that they mean only a little something by it, and they really mean a lot. It has a whine in it.

ADAM: I didn't know you were a purist.

ELEANOR: I'm not saying that I'd have a law passed about it.

ADAM: But don't you admit that it's often very difficult to know exactly the right word to use? Much more difficult than in other languages. Take French. There's always exactly the right word or expression for what you mean.

ELEANOR: No, it's the other way round. In French you have to mean exactly what the word or expression says. In English you can make your own meaning. In French you have to mean what they mean.

ADAM: Who's 'they'?

ELEANOR: The French, of course.

ADAM: But isn't it just the same in any language? In English don't you have to mean what 'they' mean?

ELEANOR: Not at all. The English aren't foreigners and English isn't a foreign language. You know, when you're thinking, how your head is full of words that you don't actually pronounce. Well, if you opened people's heads all over the world and caught the words before they actually came out, you'd find that they were all English words.

ADAM: I've never heard that version of the British Empire before. And why don't they come out English all over the world?

ELEANOR: Oh, they have adventures in the nose and throat, and the stomach, and so naturally come out Chinese or Czechoslovakian or Finnish. In English you say what you think. In other languages people say what they feel instead of what they think—it gets mixed up with the digestion and what-not.

ADAM: But look here! You don't mean that *pig* in English isn't exactly the same thing as *pig* in French? Or don't take pig, because perhaps French pigs *are* different from English pigs. Take *sky*. It's the same sky whether a Frenchman or an Englishman is looking at it.

ELEANOR: Then why do the English say *sky* and the French *ciel*?

ADAM: Oh, a matter of temperament. A French word has to have a sort of twist to it. Just like French cooking.

ELEANOR: There you are! And English words aren't twisty—they're plain English. All foreign words have a particular twist, according to the language. English words don't have twists and therefore aren't foreign. Take your word *pig*. Obviously, a pig is a *pig*. And obviously a *cochon* could only be a Frenchman's pig. Same with *boar*. A boar is a *boar*. But to a Frenchman it's a *sanglier*. Now, tell me:

is a boar a *boar* or is it a *sanglier*? Really?

ADAM: You mean what would a boar call itself?

ELEANOR: Don't be facetious. I mean in the *last analysis*.

ADAM: That's an expression I dislike as much as you dislike 'modicum.' It sounds so hopeless, like Judgement Day.

ELEANOR: Well, Judgement Day is bound to be pretty hopeless for a lot of people.

ADAM: What do you think about survival? According to evolution it's the survival of the strongest. And according to modern science it's the survival of the normalest. But, of course, there must be a different law for survival in eternity. Supposing there is such a survival—and it doesn't hurt to suppose—what kind do you think it is?

ELEANOR: I think it's the survival of the nicest.

ADAM: Whew! And is anybody really nice? I mean, fundamentally?

ELEANOR: No, of course not. Niceness doesn't mean what you are fundamentally, but making a good apology for the particular kind of horridness you suffer from.

ADAM: Oh, apologies! People are always ready with those. The worst criminals can think up the best apologies. What's all this psychoanalysis, but thinking up apologies for perverts? So-and-so is a masochist because his mother used to tickle him a lot when he was a child.

ELEANOR: I don't mean past history as an excuse

for present iniquity. That's humiliating. I mean a really good explanation.

ADAM: All right! Suppose it's Judgement Day, and I, fundamentally not a nice person, want to make a good impression. And to do this I have to give a really good explanation. What do I explain? How horrid I am, fundamentally?

ELEANOR: You tell all about yourself. Exactly what you're like. You don't call it horrid, and you don't call it nice. You give the facts and let it go at that. Stick to yourself and don't try to be anyone else. Accept yourself, with all your faults. In religion you have to accept a certain creed, and a certain god. But in the last analysis you have to accept yourself—if you want to survive. Heaven to most people means a place where they can get rid of themselves—be nicer than they are. Which makes God a universal scapegoat who takes on everybody's horridness. But *real* niceness is not disowning your own horridness. And that's what charm is—making the best of your deficiencies.

ADAM: That's very true, you know. My mother, as my father's housekeeper, had two maids to help her. One was very pretty—she was called Connie. Black hair, large blue eyes. The other was quite ugly. She had a fat nose, and hair of no particular colour, and heavy eyelids, so that her eyes seemed just slits of eyes, and, worst of all, a slanting mouth—it had been cut open at one end when she was a child, in an accident, and I suppose sewing it up had pulled it out of line. Her name was Doris. Well, strange as it may seem, Doris had real charm—while Connie just bored her young men. Of course, Doris's mouth didn't slant very badly, but it would have been an unpleasant thing to look at, and she would have been a glum, unpleasant person, if she hadn't tried to make the best of it. In fact, you could almost say that all her charm was concentrated in her mouth. And I suppose the trouble with Connie was that, being so pretty, she thought there was nothing in her that needed excusing.

ELEANOR: Yes, but if you put it that way it sounds like propaganda for facial disfigurement as a form of beauty.

ADAM: As a matter of fact, with primitive people beauty is largely a matter of facial disfigurement, isn't it? I remember seeing a film several years ago in which the women of a certain African tribe all had lips that clapped together like ducks' bills. And then they all scar their faces. And those heavy nose-rings. And you sometimes see Indian women with a tiny diamond inserted in the fleshy part of the nose. And what about moles—with women wearing black patches to imitate moles?

ELEANOR: There's no idea of disfigurement in all that. Those women had protruding lips because they really think protruding lips beautiful. Or it may have been that long ago they used to worship ducks. It often happens like that with religion—the women keep up some forgotten belief or rite. I don't mean that women are naturally conservative, but they somehow don't let men forget the past. And as for moles and patches, they emphasize the whiteness of the skin. Or else, if a woman has a mole in a certain place, it makes a man feel proud to know about it, as if in knowing about it he knew the woman's secret. A man loves to feel he knows a woman's secret—and that he alone knows it. There's that silly play of Shakespeare's, *Cymbeline*, where the wicked Italian sneaks into Imogen's bedroom and uncovers her without waking her and sees that she has a mole on one breast—I forget which. And, of course, when he tells her husband about the mole, the husband is sure that Imogen has been unfaithful to him. A man doesn't like to feel that he's sharing a woman's secret with any other man—it ceases to be a secret. And with all that fuss about it, what does the secret amount to? Just sleeping with her. Bedroom secrets.

ADAM: But *have* women a secret—a real secret?

ELEANOR: Indeed they have! And they know how to keep it. They keep it so well that men think they can master it just by sleeping with them. It's like with some mysterious island, say the Island of the Hesperides, where the golden apples grow. The apples aren't real golden apples, merely symbols that it's a pretty wonderful island. But Hercules kills the dragon and steals the apples and brings them home, thinking he's conquered the secret of the island. Every man is a sort of Hercules and sex is just a tour to foreign places. He kills the dragon, brings home the fruit, and thinks he knows it all.

ADAM: But isn't it very dishonest of women to let men think they have their secret, keeping it back all the time?

ELEANOR: Women can't prevent men from telling lies to themselves. And you don't expect women to give themselves away just because men happen to be interested in them, from selfish curiosity? Any more than you expect the natives of a country to turn themselves inside out just because foreigners condescend to say, 'How quaint!' The most you can expect from the natives is good manners—in self-protection. Which is what men get from women—good manners, and also in self-protection. And the least women can expect, in return, is good manners—instead of gloating. You don't find that gloating tone in the Bible, where people have had a vision of God. Even Moses, who saw quite a lot of God, didn't pretend to know all the secrets. 'The *secret* things belong unto the Lord our God' was the way they looked at it.

ADAM: But you don't mean to compare women with God, surely?

ELEANOR: I admit the analogy has its faults. But there's practically nothing else you can compare women with.

ADAM: What's wrong with comparing them with men?

ELEANOR: Because men are what they do and women are what they are. It always comes down to comparing a work of art with— 'And what have women to show?' And very demurely we show ourselves. Which upsets all their critical values. Much less disturbing if we keep ourselves to ourselves, and let them go on comparing themselves with themselves.

FOUR

THE NEXT DAY they happened to be interested in the greengrocer's than in anything else in the street. It was Saturday, and things always seem busier on Saturdays. And Saturday activities always seem more significant than the activities of the earlier days of the week: to-morrow the world comes to an end—for a day. What struck Eleanor was that, of the first three women she noticed going to the shop, not one was without a hat. The fourth wore no hat, but she was, from her clothes, a servant. The fifth wore a hat, and the sixth. Yet you could see that they all lived quite close, though only one came out of the houses opposite the nursing-home. To put hats on for so short a distance must mean that they didn't feel at home in the neighbourhood. They probably felt, indeed, that even their next-door neighbours were strangers. People always dressed better for strangers than for their friends or intimates, unless there was a strong sex-element, as in the first days of marriage. But then, if there was a strong sex-element it was the same thing as being strangers. Or worse: positive mistrust. With complete strangers there wasn't much mistrust. On the contrary, one felt rather friendly, in a vague way, to all strangers. *Ideally*, they were all potential friends, and one avoided knowing them in order to keep up the illusion that, if one knew them, they would certainly be friends.

Davis came out on to the veranda, just to look at the fine day for a moment. 'Now this'd be a lovely day out on the sea, or walking in the park.'

'Poor Davis,' said Adam. 'You nurses have nothing but your happy spirits.'

'And even that is acquired only after long years of study,' said Davis.

'Never mind, Davis,' said Eleanor. 'You get quite a lot of fun out of it. You can't say you don't love your work.'

'Nurses have no alternative but to love their work. They'd become murderesses if they didn't, seeing all the opportunities they have.'

'But isn't it a pleasure to see people get well?' asked Adam.

'Most people aren't half so nice when they're well as when they're ill. A person can be a roaring beast on his feet, but in the more dangerous stages of his illness he's bound to be as tame as a lamb, if only because he can't help himself.'

'And don't you feel any pity when you see a great roaring beast laid low?' asked Adam.

'Certainly not,' said Davis. 'It's good for their souls. Gives them a foretaste of the after-life, when brute strength is as dirt in God's sight.'

'Well,' said Eleanor to Davis, 'You needn't talk—you're no weakling.'

'It's no use trying to plough through the jungle of life without means of self-defence, is it now?' said Davis.

Davis was soon gone, and Eleanor and Adam, brought out of their private thoughts, went on talking.

ADAM: Don't you think there's any value in what Davis calls brute strength?

ELEANOR: Only if it's used by other people. It's awful when a person uses his brute strength for his own interests. But brute strength is all right if it's put in harness.

ADAM: Still, when you see a tiger at the Zoo, don't you admire its brute strength, objectively? You wouldn't think of putting tigers in harness?

ELEANOR: That's a very different matter. Tigers don't try to use their strength for great private ends—they don't try to become great men. They just want to be tigers.

ADAM: But surely you don't think that people can become great merely through brute strength?

ELEANOR: Certainly I do. All your so-called great men are bullies at heart. They may not go about knocking people down, but it amounts to the same thing. They do it by looks and gestures and even thoughts—hypnotism. The only difference between knocking people down and hypnotizing them is that with hypnotism you can knock down more people. And you not only knock down their bodies, but you lay their minds flat.

ADAM: You wouldn't call Einstein a bully, would you? Working with delicate mathematical symbols, or else playing his violin—you wouldn't want anyone gentler, or shyer. And yet the whole world calls him a great man. What about someone like that?

ELEANOR: Those gentle-shy ones are the most deceptive. Take music. Music is pure hypnotism. It gets hold of all your attention and then does things to you—whatever it likes. Elaborate system of magic.

ADAM: I agree that there's a good deal of magic behind many of the things that succeed. But there are all kinds of magic. Magic isn't necessarily fraudulent. And you wouldn't say, anyway, that there was magic in science?

ELEANOR: Indeed I would—science has all the earmarks of black magic. Unintelligible symbols, unintelligible formulae, and irrational results. Electric light and aeroplanes and bringing practically dead people back to life: all scientific achievements are absolutely irrational. One might even say that they are all illusions and that all scientists are illusionists. A scientist takes hold of one small fact that is true *in a way*. Then he holds it up before his audience, like any conjurer with clever hands, and says, 'Ladies and gentlemen, if you will give me all your attention I will prove to you that this fact is true in every way.' That is, by waving his little fact at you he makes you forget everything else, and so his little fact becomes the whole truth. Einstein takes hold of one small fact: that if you move off far away from yourself, from earth and commonsense and everything you know to be true and right, it all looks wrong. The further off you go, the crazier the place seems that you've left behind. But how much of a fact is it, this standing off—who really stands off like that? Einstein, perhaps, and a few other dislocated souls. But people like to feel that they're both natural and unnatural, both consistent and inconsistent. It gives them a higher, mystical consistency. And so Einstein's a great man—because he is able to make people lose their sense of balance.

ADAM: That's a rather idealized explanation of Einstein's success, because actually only a few scientists really understand his theory.

ELEANOR: An audience doesn't have to *understand* a conjurer's tricks in order to enjoy them. In fact, the less they understand, the more enjoyment they have. That other scientists understand Einstein merely means that they accept him as one of the troupe. They give him professional standing because he has a good trick and because all his successes, once they make him a member, bring credit to the profession as a whole. What, after all, is the difference between a quack and a regular doctor? A man's a quack if other doctors feel that his successes bring credit only to himself—if he refuses to say that his successes are the result of the general art of doctoring, as it is practiced by the whole troupe, rather than of his own personal brilliance.

ADAM: I don't think you credit the public with

sufficient intelligence. The public aren't such fools as you make out. Just think of the writers—think of all the trouble that they take to write the kind of thing the public will like. If they had only to do with fools, writers could make the public like anything.

ELEANOR: On the contrary, I think the public is made up of very intelligent people—most people are intelligent in one way or another. But when you take the public as a mass, as an audience, you have to deal with something besides intelligence. The first thing to consider about it then is not that it is intelligent, but that it's very sensitive. You have to consider its sensibilities. And it's the intelligent people who are the most sensitive ones. Well, first of all, writers have to be careful *not* to arouse the passions of their public. Soothe them, stroke them, make them purr a little. Once they have their readers in a semi-dormant condition, then writers can come clean and say what they really mean to say—if they have anything to say. But either they have nothing to say or, if they have, it doesn't seem worth troubling to say—the public being by this time sunk in a complaisant doze. And so this art of soothing the public becomes the whole show. The public worked into a giant purr, and there they are left. Nothing is said to them, really, and anybody is a writer who can produce a purr. Instead of new books, new ideas, new messages, all you have is new kinds of purring. Think of all the trouble writers take now in getting purry titles for their books. Instead of 'An Errand of

Love', it's 'Love's Errand'—which makes you feel inside the mystery before you start reading. Like a silly woman I know who always says: 'It's not the difference in food that makes eating in a restaurant more exciting than eating at home, but the difference in the names.' Often now the title is a whole sentence: 'A Window Is Shut' or 'A Window Is Open'. Has a nice practical sound, as if to say: '*We* don't have to stand on ceremony with each other.' Sometimes it's a quotation the public will half-know and not be able to place. It teases them and they buy the book, and the author either does the decent thing by telling them exactly where it hails from, or the flattering thing by insinuating that of course they know. And either way makes them purr. 'If Winter Comes', and so on. And 'This Freedom'. Which was followed by a lot of other 'This's'—not quotations, but 'This' had acquitted a purry foothold in the public's heart. Then there was the 'No' period—that's still going on.

ADAM: Yes—'No Castle In Spain'. And there have been a lot of 'No Strange This-or-That's'—like 'No Strange Encounter'.

ELEANOR: And there have been some 'Not's', too. And dropping the article. Instead of 'The Man Without A Heart'—'Man Without Heart'. It gives the public a respectable pornographic throb—sort of nudist. The No-Not convention came from poetry, I suppose. That's another curious thing about modern novels. They all have to be studded with poetical tit-bits—to keep up the purring. 'The moon, a gossamer incandescence, lit up his mind and his sorrow seemed a bright, happy thing.' You find writing like that in the most prosaic stories. And nobody takes it seriously, but they'd miss it if it weren't there, just as Americans get so used to all kinds of luxuries that they can't distinguish between home comforts and luxuries. And I suppose it also means that people stop reading poetry—they get enough of it in novels.

ADAM: It's a funny thing, what you call purring. It's quite the most weakening feeling I know. I get it when someone I don't know very well does nice things for me. Every time I have a new charwoman to clean my rooms, and she's friendly and competent, it comes all over me. When I get to know her it wears off. But the first few days it's very uncomfortable. Like all the parts of my brain being tucked in with little blankets. Driving very fast along a very smooth road has exactly the same effect on me. The speed puts me into a dreamy swoon. I suppose in both cases it's a sense of being carried along one doesn't know quite where. People who are continually surrounded by lots of servants must always be in that purry state.

ELEANOR: No one is *always* surrounded by lots of servants, not even the richest or most important people. Even kings and queens and princes must have their private moments.

ADAM: I can't imagine a royal personage feeling anything but public all the time. You don't expect a king or a queen to have a private life any more than you expect

God to. You know they go to bed and have bathrooms and so on, but there must be very little *said* between them that couldn't be repeated in public. It may all be a question of wives. The higher up you go the less difference you find between husbands and wives—it's a sign of aristocracy. The more difference there is, the more things to be intimate about. That's why, I suppose, you find a tendency in the sons of earls to marry chorus girls: they hunger for the kind of familiarity and foolish chat they can't enjoy with women of their own class.

ELEANOR: Nonsense! Do you mean that there's more difference of personality between lower-class husbands and wives than between upper-class husbands and wives? And so spicier repartee? Ever listened to lower-class conversation?

ADAM: Ever listened to upper-class conversation? Any particular remark or story or observation might be made equally by any one of the talkers: all the same voice, male or female, old or young, solemn or gay. It all sounds so intelligent—and so insincere.

ELEANOR: You wouldn't exactly call our conversation lower-class, would you? And I don't think we're insincere.

ADAM: I'd call it convalescent. You wouldn't exactly call yourself upper-class, would you?

ELEANOR: Of course I would! You wouldn't call me lower-class, would you?

ADAM: No, but I should think we're both fairly complete middle-class types.

ELEANOR: The middle class is a myth. Real people are either upper or lower, just as they're either female or male. In fact, you might call the lower class the masculine one and the upper class the feminine one. The lower class has all the male vices and virtues and the upper class all the female vices and virtues. People are born one thing or the other. You don't find many lower-class types born in the upper class, but it happens. You find more and more upper-class types born in the lower class. But there's no such thing as a middle-class *type*. The middle class consists of—well, of people who never feel quite at home in the world. They die, but they don't live. It's like a graveyard. It's the people who don't go either to heaven or hell when they die—they just go to their graves. They don't trouble to develop a character, and so nothing ever happens to them. All the drama in life is either in the upper or the lower class, or between the two classes.

ADAM: How is it, then, that the middle class is called the backbone of the Empire? Think of London. It's largely made up of shops. And it's the middle class that keeps the shops.

ELEANOR: Don't you believe it. The mean little shops are kept by the working class. At closing-hour they're as tired as any rough labourer. That's the real test of what class you belong to—how tired you are at the end of the day. The bigger shops are full of lower-class employees with upper-class bosses who aren't tired at the end of the day. And then the jobs in the big shops get divided into lower-class and upper-class jobs.

ADAM: Where does the middle class come in, then? Who *is* middle-class?

ELEANOR: All the failures. A lower-class person doesn't consider whether he's a failure or not—he merely gets on with his job, accepts himself through his job. And an upper-class person is automatically a success because he's pleased with himself—takes it for granted that he's charming and important, since that's how he honestly feels about himself. It's very difficult to say exactly who is middle-class, but in general it's the people you don't either like or dislike strongly. They just hover about, semi-irritating, and semi-irritated with themselves. Whereas, with lower-class and upper-class people, you either definitely like or definitely dislike them.

ADAM: Wouldn't it be wonderful if there were *one* book in which you could find all the right answers to all the questions? For example, you give what sounds a very plausible explanation of class divisions. But I wouldn't take it as gospel truth, and nobody would, no matter how plausible it sounded. Even if you wrote it down in a book. People would say—and I'd say, 'What's your authority?' And where is there any authority?

ELEANOR: Yes. If I appeared before you in a white robe and spoke in a husky solemn voice you'd be more likely to take what I said as sound, no matter what rot I talked. That'd make *you* feel important, and so I'd be an authority. People only believe in what makes them feel important. A nice complicated person who talks to them in a nice complicated language won't do. Oh, no. It's got to be some inspired idiot who speaks in a confused enough way to make it possible for them to pretend they understand without having to explain what sense they make of it. Everyone, including the inspired idiot, secure in his knowing look because each is afraid to challenge the other.

ADAM: But you wouldn't say that you really knew about things?

ELEANOR: I know enough. Any woman knows quite enough.

ADAM: Then you think women know more than men?

ELEANOR: Any woman knows enough to answer any question a man is likely to ask her.

ADAM: Come, come! You wouldn't say you could answer all the questions put to you by the wisest man in the world?

ELEANOR: The wisest man in the world would consider it beneath his dignity to ask questions of women. That saves us a lot of time. The so-called wise men ask themselves questions. First they think up the answers, and then they suit their questions to the answers. That's called genius. Every genius is an intellectual Narcissus. Closed corporation.

ADAM: But isn't it a good thing for people to be self-sufficient? Especially since there is no reliable central authority to go to for advice? If no one was able to make up his own mind, the world would be just a gigantic traffic-jam. You know how it is sometimes in a crowded street. One person not sure whether he wants to pass you on the right or on the left can cause a lot of confusion. Not only does he fuss you, but you fuss the people near you because you, too, hesitate for a moment, not sure exactly what's going to happen.

ELEANOR: And is it so serious if he does run into me? Wouldn't he be very sorry, and apologize, and wouldn't I smile prettily?

ADAM: Yes, but suppose there was a lot of it? Would you go on smiling? Would everybody else?

ELEANOR: On the other hand, what makes it possible to go through life, and through crowded streets, but the fact that most people aren't absolutely sure of the next step? And what makes conversation possible, but the fact that no one is absolutely sure what he is going to say next, or what the other person is going to say? If everyone were quite deliberate about what he was going to do next, it'd all end soon enough—in a universal war. As it is, we go on fairly slowly, and by degrees come to realize that the only way to progress is to stop and think.

ADAM: That reminds me of a story my mother used to tell us when we had been naughty during the day. It was supposed to be a punishment, hearing it over and over again, but we never got tired of it: it was more like a reward for being naughty. It was about two children,

Isabel and Kenneth, who were sent by their father on a very important errand. The father was a jeweller, and there was a precious jewel to deliver to a rich Indian Prince. The regular errand-boy happened to be away for the day with a severe cold, and their father had to watch the shop, and their mother had her housework to attend to. The jewel had to be delivered that very day because the Prince was going back to India and would certainly not miss his boat for a mere jewel; he had thousands of jewels, many more beautiful and precious than this one, which he wanted only to carry in his pocket carelessly, to show to people, saying, I suppose, 'This worthless trifle can give you no idea whatever of my real treasures.' But at any rate it cost quite a lot of money, and the father had received a large deposit for it, and as he was an honest man he didn't want the Prince to lose his money. So the father decided to send it by Isabel and Kenneth. 'No one will imagine that you are carrying anything valuable,' he said, 'because you are only children. But if anything goes wrong, just stop and think, no matter how frightened you are.' And when they asked what they were to think, the father said, 'Just stop and think and remember that you are only children.'

Well, Isabel, being the elder, had the address of the Prince's hotel in her pocket, while Kenneth had the jewel in his. And Isabel also had the bus fares and a little over. The father reasoned that the address and the bus fares should be put in charge of the wiser head, because it didn't take much sense to keep a thing in one's pocket but a lot of sense to get somewhere safely. And he didn't want to hold Isabel responsible for the jewel as well, because too much responsibility makes even the wisest heads nervous. So off they went, with the responsibility divided in this way between them. The jewel lay loose in Kenneth's right-hand pocket. His father thought it best not to wrap it up in anything, because every time Kenneth felt it he would remember immediately what it was; and he thought the right-hand pocket best because this was the one Kenneth naturally put his hand into most.

Don't laugh at me for telling it so nicely. We all knew if off by heart. Often my mother used to make us pick it up at a certain point and carry it on. Especially when she came to the crisis, where they had to stop and think.

ELEANOR: It's one of the nicest stories I've ever heard. Do go on. I love a story with a crisis in it. In life there's rarely a crisis, unless it's a tragedy, and there are so few real tragedies.

ADAM: I always think there's a lot of tragedy in life, but that people have to make a joke of their troubles because no one is interested in them but themselves.

ELEANOR: No, I don't agree. People don't take things seriously enough. To have tragedy everyone concerned has to be in dead earnest. That's what I like about children's stories—you get a sort of dead-earnestness. There has to be a dead-earnestness behind them for children to be interested. Children take everything *so* seriously, if it's only going to buy sweets or playing with a toy train. And when you call a grown-up person childish, isn't that what you mean? That he takes everything too seriously? When you're a child you have so many values—this is good, and that, and that. And then as you grow up you bring it down to about one value because you decide that you can't hope for everything. But do go on, I'm dying to come to the crisis where they have to stop and think. I suppose by now they're in a bus and well on their way to the magnificent hotel where the disgustingly rich Indian Prince lives. Was he disgustingly wicked, too? Is he going to kidnap the children and take them to India and make them into little heathens who ride elephants and sacrifice all their pennies to Buddha?

ADAM: You look too far ahead. In a children's story you mustn't let your imagination run away with you. You have to be more or less sensible, no matter how silly the original idea is.

Well, as you say, by now they were sitting on the top of a bus and on their way. They had to change the bus from No. 93 or something to bus No. 14 or something. When they had been riding for about ten minutes in the second bus Isabel began to say to herself, 'I wonder if this is really the right bus?' Her father had said to her, 'Above all, don't ask people questions if anything goes wrong. It'll make them get interested and wonder what two children are doing out alone by themselves.' So she decided that the best thing to do would be to get off. Once they were off the bus, she saw that it had been No. 17 and not No. 14. What were they to do? How were they to find bus No. 14? She and Kenneth stopped and thought and remembered, of course, that they were only children. This made them think, also, that too much couldn't be expected of children. And, as they found themselves just outside a park, they decided to go inside and sit down and rest for a bit. Isabel bought two cakes from a man who stood at the entrance of the park selling things, and they went and sat down and ate them.

'Is the jewel safe?' Isabel asked. Kenneth took it out of his pocket and showed it to her, grinning. They both felt pleased that the jewel was safe and went on sitting for some time. Then they got up and walked through the park, coming out on the other side. It was a much grander neighbourhood on this side, with large houses in which wealthy people lived. And naturally no buses came here. So they walked on, and, feeling tired again, sat down on a door-step. A very kind-looking old man came out of the house and spoke to them and invited them to come inside to drink some chocolate. Their mouths were dry after the cakes and they wanted to accept the kind old man's invitation. But first Isabel stopped to think. 'We are only children,' she said to herself, 'and kind old people who live in grand houses don't do horrible things to children.' So they accepted the invitation. And soon they were sitting in chairs as soft as beds, and a butler with manners as smooth as a clergyman's was giving them chocolate mostly made of cream. After that they didn't know what to do, because, although they realized that they ought to be getting on their way, they didn't want to offend the kind old man hurrying off too soon. So they sat and smiled at him, and he smiled back at them. Then finally Isabel said, 'I think we must go now, because we have to find a certain Indian Prince.'

She knew that it was dangerous to confide such an important secret to a perfect stranger, but she thought, 'Well, I am only a child. It is all so difficult and I must confide in someone.' Fortunately, she had confided in just the right person, because the kind old man asked her *what* Indian Prince, and she showed him the paper in her pocket, and it turned out that the kind old man knew him quite well. 'We'll all go there together,' he said, 'for I was planning to pay him a visit myself some time today, to bid him good-bye.' And he told the butler to tell the chauffeur to get the car ready. Kenneth was so excited at the idea of everything's turning out so well that he dropped the jewel on the carpet. The kind old man picked it up and whistled softly to himself when he saw what it was and said, 'Perhaps you had better let me take care of this for you.' It made them a little nervous, but Isabel decided that things had gone so far already that they had better let Providence take its course. Children could not do more than that. So off they went, in the most luxurious car, and here, too, the seats were as soft as beds. And soon they were at the hotel where the Prince lived, and being introduced to him by the kind old man, who now carefully gave the jewel back to Kenneth for him to hand to the Prince.

Then the Prince gave Kenneth the rest of the money due for the jewel, but the kind old man interrupted and said, 'Perhaps you had better let me take care of this for you.' And then all three said good-bye to the Prince, who was a handsome, wicked-looking man with very elegant manners, and off they went again in the kind old man's car. He took them back to their father's shop, and their father wasn't at all angry, since things had turned out so well, and he and the kind old man became fast friends. And the moral of it all was that children were to stop and think and remember that they were only children. It was a wise way of punishing us, really, because, knowing it was meant as a punishment, we used to listen very soberly, and there was no unpleasant reaction, as there generally is after one's been punished. And it was such a nice story that it made us feel we were forgiven, and generally we used to go straight to sleep after it, which was also good for us.

Eleanor was asleep; Adam was exhausted. How long Davis had left them out this morning! Miss Kenwood came toward them, followed by Davis: she had passed their rooms and seen that their beds were empty. She was angry, although anger made no perceptible difference in her manner. She merely said a little less than usual. Davis explained: 'I thought, it being such a lovely day, and so warm, and they seem to enjoy it—'

'You are not supposed to use your judgement, except in emergencies,' said Miss Kenwood. 'A warm day is not an emergency. Patients should have at least a half-hour's rest *in bed* before lunch.'

Eleanor woke and smiled at Miss Kenwood and at Adam and at Davis. Nobody smiled back.

'You will give them their lunches after everybody else has been served,' said Miss Kenwood.

It sounded like a punishment, but Eleanor did not care. It was such a nice story, and she knew exactly what the Indian Prince looked like, though the kind old man was a little dim.

FIVE

ON THEIR SIXTH MORNING together Eleanor and Adam began by feeling rather irritated with each other. Trebble was somewhat to blame, but the real reason was that they were getting used to being together. The expansive blandness of new friendship was gradually wearing down to a more natural intimacy; and when people first become old friends they are likely to behave more rudely to each other than when they are very old friends. That is, there had been a quarrel; and the excuse was something Trebble had said to Eleanor about something Adam had said to her about Eleanor. It was when Trebble was mixing Eleanor's mouth-wash. She always saw to Adam first because he did not resent being awakened early, and Eleanor did.

'Number Seventeen has just been telling me that you would make a good champion of the position of women in the world,' Trebble said.

'Me!' said Eleanor, waking up. 'But I'm not a champion of anything. What made him say that? Do I look like a champion? Champions have grim expressions on their faces and dress badly.'

'You're certainly not one of those manly types, though

I've only seen you in your nightgown. But he caught me sighing, and he said, "Poor Trebble, you women get all the worst jobs." And I said, "We bring it on ourselves," and he said, "Can't anything be done about it—can't all you women get together—choose a leader?" And I said, "There's few of us that thinks further than getting a little peace now and then." And isn't it the truth? Take those suffragettes, with all they suffered for the Cause—what was the Cause? Votes and equal rights, which is to say that in our spare moments we are supposed to feel happier because we have teased the men into saying we are just as capable of making mistakes as they are. But personally, when I'm off duty all I want is a little peace and not to think about new laws and ideas that don't make things better for me personally—somebody's got to do the nursing.'

Eleanor had by this time rinsed her mouth, washed her face, combed her hair and put on a wooly bed-jacket. 'But where do I come in? What exactly did Number Seventeen say about me?'

'He said,' Trebble answered, giving Eleanor her tea, 'that you were a woman who could if you liked make the world see different about a lot of things, by going around quietly and saying what *you* thought. He said there must be many intelligent women like you, not fanatics but just sensible, who could wake people up if they weren't so lazy.'

'Who'd he say was lazy.' asked Eleanor, sitting up

suspiciously, 'me or people?'

'I think he meant you—but he meant no offence, he meant it broadly, thinking about the need of champions, and like me not being in sympathy with the aggressive type.'

'So I'm one of those mild-mannered little fairies who could do it all with a wave of my wand, but I'm too lazy to raise my arm? Men will talk the most long-winded nonsense, merely from a desire to see how far they can go without being interrupted or corrected. They're never sure whether what they say is right or true, but that makes no difference to the positiveness with which they express themselves.'

'But you say things in a positive way, don't you, Miss Five? Aren't we all, man, woman or child, entitled to our beliefs and to speak our minds?'

'I never speak my mind unless I'm quite sure beforehand that I'm in the right,' said Eleanor.

'But how is anyone to know if she's in the right or not?' asked Trebble. 'Not all of us has brains like yours.'

'Everybody has brains, Trebble, just as everybody has a heart and a stomach and so on. It's not brains that make people talk sense or nonsense, but character. A person with a pleasant character can't help talking sense. And your character isn't a part of your body, it's how you mix the various parts. It's like cooking. You can either throw things together anyhow and make a mess, or by taking pains you can produce, with the identical materials, something really good to eat.'

'Yes, but all the same,' Trebble said, 'it takes a knowledge of words to talk the way you do, no matter how pleasant their character is. Words are the same as the plates and serviettes and cutlery and all the things that make the best-cooked meal a loss if they're not there.'

ADAM: It's like watching fate—seeing people going into a post-office, get stamps, and come out and drop their letters in the pillarbox. And every one of them walks away with a nervous little jaunt. Suppose people didn't write letters. But it's one of those Temptations, like speaking to strangers in a railway compartment.

ELEANOR: Or talking at random to nurses about fellow-patients.

ADAM: Oh, Trebble's been saying things—that's why you're cross!

ELEANOR: I'm not cross: I'm angry. What right have you to make sweeping statements about me to a simple-minded person like Trebble?

ADAM: One can only make sweeping statements to simple-minded people, especially at six o'clock in the morning.

ELEANOR: Need you make sweeping statements at six o'clock in the morning?

ADAM: It's a very good time for making them. Later on in the day one gets careful. And in the evening one says practically nothing. You're invited out to dinner and the whole object is to say practically nothing, or you stay at home and read and let the author do all the talking. Anyway, why all this fuss because I praise you to Trebble? You're not sacred, are you?

ELEANOR: No, I'm not sacred, but I reserve the right to make my own reputation.

ADAM: There's no such thing as a self-made reputation. That's what friends—and enemies—are for. They talk about you, and you get known. The public doesn't believe in people who aren't talked about. It's not what a person writes or does or is that make him famous, but what's said about him, from mouth to mouth. Like with Christ. He got himself talked about. His whole reputation is based on rumour.

ELEANOR: You sound like a publicity agent arguing with a shy author. That's not quite my position. I'm someone you met in a nursing-home and you're someone I met in a nursing-home, and that's the end of it.

ADAM: I hope not. I was just beginning to get used to your little peculiarities. It'd be a pity if it were all wasted.

ELEANOR: I'm sorry the experience has been so painful.

ADAM: Well, you're making it rather painful this morning. I'm sure it's bad for both of us for you to be in such a bad temper.

ELEANOR: You talk as if I were a nursing mother, and you the child.

ADAM: I must say I feel very close to you in a lot of

ways. For instance, I actually enjoy your being angry with me. Makes a pleasant family background. One doesn't get angry with complete strangers.

ELEANOR: In fact, we're as good as married to each other.

ADAM: Or else I'm a child at your bosom.

ELEANOR: Don't be disgusting.

ADAM: You don't think motherhood is disgusting, do you?

ELEANOR: Everything's disgusting if you make it personal.

ADAM: Isn't that a rather sweeping statement at eleven o'clock in the morning?

ADAM: Now, I'm sure that was the same woman.

ELEANOR: What woman?

ADAM: First she went into the greengrocer's, then I saw her coming out of the post-office, then I saw her going into the post-office again, about ten minutes ago—and she hasn't come out yet. And I'm sure she's not in there now, and I've been watching very carefully, and I'm sure it's the same woman. And yet it couldn't be.

ELEANOR: It probably is the same woman. There aren't so many people in the world as the statistics say. A lot of so-called people are just duplicates. There are so many, many duplicates and triplicates that it's very difficult to find the originals.

ADAM: Do you mean like reincarnation—that there

are many people who are exactly the same as people who have lived before?

ELEANOR: That happens, too, but not so simply, because it also happens that many people are echoes of people alive in the same time with them, as well as being echoes of people who lived before them. It's very confusing—like knowing whether a book is really good or not. It's so easy to throw a book together and make it seem all right, with echoes of this and echoes of that—until you can hardly tell the real thing from the imitation. That's what critics are supposed to be for. But, as most of them are only echoes themselves, how can they know? And God is supposed to be able to do the same with people; but after all, isn't God a conglomeration of echoes of people? How can one only rely on God's judgements any more than one can on the critics'? And at least the critics go on trying, but it's a long time since God has said anything new.

ADAM: It's funny how people are beginning to talk about God again. I can remember the time when people used either to believe or not believe. But now they neither believe nor disbelieve, they just talk. And it's not skepticism, but defeatism, just as people get resigned to their mothers and fathers and grandparents—not sisters and brothers, because one doesn't really get resigned to them. People seem now to accept the idea of God the way they accept their psychological make-up and all their Freudian bad habits—as if he were a very interesting bad habit.

CONVALESCENT CONVERSATIONS

I once asked some people, sitting around talking, how they thought of God. They were all quite sophisticated people, and I'm sure not one of them had been inside a church for years, but not one of them laughed at me for asking such a question or said he didn't think of God in any shape or form. Each of them gave a very conscientious answer, and all the answers were nicely detailed, like memories of something naughty you did when you were a child. One saw God as a queer mandarin fellow with a tiny yellow face, wearing a yellow satin robe with a lot of brownish scroll-work on it, and a hat with a turned-up brim like Spanish priests wear, only white, and squatting in the middle of a table. And another saw God as a large fixed ball with a chromium finish, too large to fit into a house, but very small in outdoor scenery—something like a shiny spot that interfered a little with vision. And another said that she always saw God as a blue sky, but not natural blue sky, more like a feeling of something blue you were floating in—and that warm, soapy bath-water, if the bath was very full and you didn't look at it, gave her the same feeling. And another said that he saw God as a great ball-room lit with dazzling lights, and millions of people dancing, people with strange faces and strange clothes, and himself standing awkwardly in the middle— the man, not God—not dancing because he wasn't a good dancer. And one woman said that she thought of God as a large hole you stepped into when you died, never touching the bottom.

ELEANOR: And how do you think of God?

ADAM: I seem to have two different pictures. One is a long stretch of wide marble steps with a female orchestra playing at the top conducted by some sturdy little mysterious fellow like Napoleon, the women in voluptuous low-necked dresses, and little naked babies crawling all over the steps. That's the Freudian one, though it isn't nasty, really—more like a coloured print commemorating some World Fair. The other picture isn't so easy to describe. It's more—what shall I say—primitive. And it varies. Sometimes it's a tremendous block of stone, much higher than a mountain. Not a thing to climb, because there's no top to it—I mean no grade: it's just a great block. The idea seems to be that there's something inside of it that would clear up all my problems; and yet I know there's nothing inside but more stone; and yet I go on standing there in front of it, trying to see into it. Then other times it's all kinds of bad weather in one—snow and hail and rain and thunder and wind, and I'm out in it, running around wild, trying to find the cause of all the trouble, or maybe a little island of good weather somewhere in it. But there's nothing but just me and this awful weather. I don't mean exactly that God's the bad weather; but he certainly isn't the little island of good weather I can't find. Somehow, he's the whole situation.

ELEANOR: You mean that your serious idea of God—not the inherited coloured-print one but the personal one—is feeling at a loss about something, and not knowing quite about what?

ADAM: Yes, that's it! Is that yours, too?

ELEANOR: I don't have ideas or pictures about God. God to me is a name—a name for all the most important things that nobody can define, and not the right name.

ADAM: You mean things like truth and goodness and reality?

ELEANOR: Yes, things like that—all the impressive ideas that people don't believe in privately, but only in groups. Or perhaps privately they believe in them a little. Then you throw a lot of people together and they believe in such things in a big way. That's what churches are for: you get people together and add up all the fractions of belief or interest that each one has in things which don't bother them very much in their daily lives—and the answer is 'God'. But no single person has more than a fraction of interest, and so the combined feeling isn't very strong—only louder; like when a schoolmaster gets the whole class to recite a poem because no single boy recites it with much enthusiasm. He gets more volume from the class as a whole, but not more enthusiasm.

ADAM: But that's not a very fair comparison. You know how boys hate poetry—makes them feel like fools. The thing schoolboys are most suspicious of is demonstrativeness. If a chap shows strong feeling about something, the others think he's putting it on. It's a sort of modesty, and it ought to be respected. People are shy about God, individually, because it's a very big idea for one small human being to face alone. And naturally they feel more comfortable when they face it together. But take your class of boys reciting a poem—each of them still feels a fool, only he doesn't mind so much because everybody else is making a fool of himself. I remember what a shameful experience it was for me when I had to write an essay on Wordsworth's daffodil poem—tell what it meant to me. And the English master chose mine as the best and *read it out* to the class. About feeling lonely as a cloud—lonely and yet lighthearted, I explained: how well I knew that feeling. For days afterwards, whenever they met me out alone, it was 'lonely and yet lighthearted.' And every time I laughed at a joke it was 'A poet could not but be gay In such a jocund company.' A poet can make a fool of himself, writing like that, and it doesn't seem to matter; but normal people shouldn't be expected to imitate him. And nobody's more normal than a schoolboy.

ELEANOR: I should say schoolboys were a lot of morbid little prigs.

ADAM: And what about schoolgirls?

ELEANOR: Oh, they're just little mice, scampering about with secrets too big for their size—so important, and so frightened.

ADAM: I once had a little girl friend who was exactly like that. She used to get me to run away with her to what she called 'a cave'—it was really just a rather dirty place behind a rock at the end of the village where people threw rubbish—and whisper the dullest things to me as if they were State Secrets; such as that she'd heard her mother telling my mother that her father had been waking up every night *sweating with excitement*. And I'd have to look very mysterious, and we were both supposed to have some deep silent understanding of this—which was supposed to mean that we were in love.

ELEANOR: Well, that's what being in love amounts to, doesn't it? Two people each indulging the other's vanity, and the whole world is their particular secret—nobody else really understands anything. And if you happen to overhear their confidences, it's all so trivial and commonplace. But, of course, everything they say is supposed to mean much more than what it sounds like. And it's the same if you happen to overhear the conversation of important people—that's really a sort of love-affair, too. And then most people have love-affairs like that with themselves—I've always wanted to spy on people, see how they behave when they're alone, how they look, what they do with their hands. I used to spy on my mother, who was very clever at seeming an important person. I'd watch and watch, and nothing interesting'd ever happen, no radiant look, or stretching out her arms—except that all of a sudden she'd scratch herself somewhere.

SIX

ELEANOR: There's the best argument against aeroplanes you could possibly find: everybody looking up. When motor-cars came in people must have looked every time one passed. But they didn't have to look up. Eyes are where they are, on the front part of the head, not too far up, for very good reasons. We stand up straight in the world we're in, and so our eyes work on the vertical principle. Even the eyes and heads of animals, who are built somewhat on horizontal lines, conform to the vertical principle. But once you have things in the world that jerk your head into the horizontal if you want to see them, you can be sure they're against nature and sanity and the logic of the body. It isn't as if there were trees and things growing in the air, or places to go to with people living in them. There's *nothing*. All this talk about air-mindedness merely means that people can't face the realities of the world they live in. Up they go, and up we gape. Well, when they're up they're out of the world. And when we gape up at them we're as good as dead for the moment. What happens when people die? Their minds and bodies snap into the horizontal, and their eyes gape up. Just as no real thinking is ever done in bed. Dreams are a very good example of what goes on in the horizontal.

ADAM: And what about birds? Surely, when you see a bird sail easily through the air, that's one of the most natural things in the world? You can't arbitrarily exclude birdlife from nature.

ELEANOR: Why can't I? Nature is what has to do with the earth, and what belongs to the earth. Birds are neither one thing nor the other. They'd like not to belong to the earth, and they go sailing off grandly to nowhere, but sooner or later down they come—to sleep, eat and reproduce their kind.

ADAM: But looking at flying just practically, why should it be so monstrous to find a way to get to places more quickly—places on earth? We do all sorts of things to simplify life intelligently, and it seems to me this is just one more—if it can be done successfully. I don't see that you can judge it by any other standard: if they get aeroplanes to work so that they're as safe as other means of travel, then they're an excellent means of travel, since they take us to places in a much shorter time than any other means. You're not just standing up for the wear-and-tear and inconveniences of the ordinary means of travel, are you? Like all those hand-weavers who still go on. Hours and hours on a very few yards of material that turns out rough and loose and stretchy and grim-looking, and costs like anything—when you can get the loveliest, neatest, cheerfullest kind of machine-made material, yards and yards of it, in every imaginable shade and texture, and quite cheap. And you know that the people who have made it haven't been working drearily day after day on one lonely square of cloth. They've had the satisfaction of feeling that lots of nice things were being made—and things to like without any of that awesome feeling you're supposed to summon up when someone whispers the word 'hand-woven.'

ELEANOR: You talk as if I were arguing for hand-woven railway trains or something. I quite agree that some people have a sickly cultured reaction to things that are obviously more sensible than old-fashioned ways—really meaning that they are too weak-minded to grasp all the intricacies of modern life. I'm not old-fashioned or weak-minded; I don't say aeroplanes are vulgar. On the contrary, I say they're not sensible. I like pleasant, convenient travelling, and slick fittings in hotel bathrooms, and the most mundane kind of improvements, such as stainless steel and moving staircases. But I don't consider aeroplanes an improvement, because the results aren't real—just as artificial silk can never be silk. Suppose you cure somebody by magic, instead of considering sensibly the nature of the disease, and giving him medicine that actually gets at the diseased part. Well, I say that you don't really cure him. And so with all this speeding up of things you get by aeroplanes: I say it doesn't mean anything, and doesn't really speed up anything—at least not anything of any importance. Unless you think it's important to be able to lunch in London and have tea in Moscow on the same day. Of course, magic can be effective in a few very special emergency cases, and that's why primitive people were so good at it, because they only used it for emergency cases. But if it becomes a general rule it ceases to be effective. And aeroplanes aren't even clever magic. Real magic can't depend on motors and the weather and anything like mechanical ability, such as pilots have to have. Real magic isn't visible; you can't crane your necks and see it happen. It's something impossible. And aeroplanes try to make impossible things happen in a rational way. And it can't be done. The only result is that you have a lot of irrational things flying about clumsily overhead, and a lot of irrational things happening all over the earth that are supposed to be rational. If people want to be like birds, why don't they get up off their legs and fly?

ADAM: You might as well say it's all wrong to use boats and trains and cars.

ELEANOR: No. They carry on normal traditions. They don't belong to 'the future'—and aeroplanes will always belong to the future, along with Esperanto and improved bodies.

ADAM: Don't you think it's possible for people to develop, by sheer will, remarkable powers of body?

ELEANOR: No, I don't. Because people haven't—not since they've been people. The only kind of development there is is mental. When people try to develop remarkable powers of body the chief result is mental decline.

Look at acrobats—what's the result of an acrobat's being able to leap from a platform into the air and hang on with his teeth to a little rope thrown to him by a kind strong lady standing on another platform? The result is that he's a fool to trust her and she's a fool to save his life at the expense of twisting all her organs out of position in the effort. The sensible thing would be for her to let go of the rope—then there'd be only one fool, and he a dead one.

ADAM: Have you ever looked at your insides through one of those transparent machines doctors put you into? You look down and see yourself coursing through all parts of your body.

ELEANOR: No, and I wouldn't like it. I don't think one ought to have a scientific interest in oneself. Spoils all one's confidence in oneself as an individual. One amoeba is just as good as another under the microscope.

ADAM: All the same, it doesn't do you any harm to know that the diagrams in the physiology books really do apply to you. Otherwise, when you have a pain, you imagine that it's a major universal event, instead of some quite trivial incident in an out-of-the-way corner of *your* world. Uncivilized peoples think that if they have a pain in the stomach it's caused by an octopus or something. And if you take a good look at yourself you see there's no room for an octopus. But a lot of people deliberately cultivate ignorance in order to have something to worry about. They forget, if they ever knew, the real cause of their troubles. If someone has high blood-pressure he goes around saying it until it means that he's pressed down by some dismal responsibility on behalf of the world in general. And it's worse if it's some Latin or Greek word, like 'anemia'—that means he's enfeebled by his sensitiveness to some tragic aspect of life to which the rest of humanity is blind. But if he had a clear picture of exactly what was wrong with him, he'd never dare to dramatize it mysteriously, unless he was a downright liar. And lack of information tempts people to be liars. For instance, declaring you have an octopus inside of you because something hurts.

ELEANOR: That's like saying that if people knew their geography and astronomy thoroughly they'd have a complete understanding of the universe. What good does all the information that scientists accumulate really do? What do they really *know*? They know how things behave, but do they know what things *mean*? And if you don't know what things mean, no matter how much information you may have about them, you play a stranger's part in life. You're just the audience, and the only thing that interests you is the setting, and what the actors wear, and which are the men and which the women, and who goes out or comes in, stands up or sits down, and noticing that this one looks angry and that one pleased. But as for what's *happening*—you might as well be at home, reading a play that consists only of stage directions. And as for a pain being an octopus—why is it truer to describe it in medical terms that tell where it is, and what particular action of the body causes it, but say nothing at all about what it feels like? If it feels like an octopus, it has the same kind of meaning to you that an octopus has—fear and clutching tentacles and a horrible squeezed sensation. And it seems much truer to say that the cause is an octopus than to place the responsibility on something the body does itself. The body doesn't really cause anything—it has feelings. And what causes the feelings isn't anything simple you can put your finger on, like a diagram in a physiology book. A cause is—well, it's more like an octopus.

'I'm awfully sorry,' Nurse Davis whispered over Eleanor's shoulder, 'but somebody else is coming out. It's the lady from Number Ten—Mrs. Lyley. But she's a dear—unless you're a heartless intellectual.'

'And do you think we're heartless intellectuals?' Adam asked.

'Well, I shouldn't like to pass judgement before listening attentively to your conversation for several hours, and my duties prevent me from confirming my suspicions. But there seems to be an awful lot of conversation.'

'And does that prove us to be heartless intellectuals?' Eleanor asked. 'What do you expect conversations to be made up of, if not conversation?'

'Oh, there could be some smiling, and some shaking of the head, and some looking into each other's eyes, and then some looking the other way and looking back again, and odds and ends of sounds like grunts, chuckles and now and then a sigh. You know what I mean—not all tongue.'

Miss Kenwood appeared at the door of the veranda. 'Nurse Davis,' she said, 'what are you doing? Performing some professional task—or just talking?'

'Performing a professional task,' Eleanor said, as Davis withdrew with an air of happy resignation to whatever opinion Miss Kenwood might form of the matter. 'She was explaining to us the nature of good conversation— telling us that our conversation wasn't very good because we talked too much.'

'I suppose you do have quite a lot to say to each other. When two people are thrown together accidentally it's the only healthy way of making the time pass. Better than falling in love and exchanging long silent looks, like a pair of invalids.'

'Well, there still might be some danger of that,' said Adam, 'seeing that we still are, technically, invalids. But we do our best.'

'If you can keep it up for three days more,' said Miss Kenwood to Adam, 'you're saved.'

'And what do you mean by that?' asked Eleanor reproachfully.

'I mean that a woman is vaguely fond of everyone, from the start. But it's the man who turns this harmless motherly feeling into romantic mischief, by persuading the woman that she's exclusively interested in him. And the result is that he's devoured. And all because of vanity.'

'I know better than to flatter myself that Number Five could possibly have more than a motherly interest in Number Seventeen,' Adam said. 'I'm a mere man-doll in her sight. And in three days, as you say, I'll be thrown aside like a plaything that no longer charms.'

'If you're so sure of that, why do you want my address?' asked Eleanor.

'Oh, just a matter of routine. History goes on, though people die. Just as Miss Kenwood will keep our records, when we've gone away to other illnesses, other nursing-homes.'

'Yes,' said Miss Kenwood, 'it's good for the stationery trade. And then there's the hope that one day there'll be no more to record.'

'And the stationery trade, and all the other trades?' asked Adam. 'Who'll there be to buy things?'

'And who'll there be to make things to buy?' said Eleanor. 'Don't you see—everyone will be just a character in the story. There won't be any life—just a story.'

'And no one to read the story,' said Adam. 'We'll all be absorbed in it. How painfully abstract.'

'But think how painfully concrete everything is now,' said Miss Kenwood.

'Oh dear, oh dear,' said Adam. 'I could burst into tears.'

'Well, here comes little Mrs. Lyley—she'll cheer you up. Life is just a few simple facts to her—and the rest the bilious fabrications of minds like ours.'

Davis was wheeling Mrs. Lyley toward them.

ELEANOR: Do you mean your husband willfully endangers his life every Sunday?

MRS. LYLEY: Oh, I suppose he has a sort of faith in his luck—he always was lucky in a small way, and he's not a man to go in for big things. That's how he's made his money and kept it. And as I was saying, every Sunday morning he goes out in this sail-boat, and he never did understand the ways of the wind, and he never will, and he never was of a mechanical turn of mind. But somehow I don't worry. He's not a young man any more, and he's led a quiet, plodding sort of life, and if he should drown himself there's a neat pile for his family, and I think it gives him a feeling of being young again and not belonging to us—though on dry land you wouldn't want a kinder husband or father. And the funny part of it is that every time he goes off a feeling of calm comes over me, and I'm sure the same kind of feeling comes over him. I feel, 'What's the use of worrying?' He's a human being, and I'm a human being, and we're all human beings, and there's not much difference between one and another, no matter how fond we may be of them—and I'm certainly as fond of my husband as any wife could be.

ADAM: But if one day he didn't come back, and his drowned body was brought home to you, surely you wouldn't be calm then? That wouldn't be human, either.

MRS. LYLEY: Oh, no. I'd cry over him, and

remember how kind and patient and hardworking he'd always been, and think how sad it was that we'd never talk things over in private again, but I think I'd feel sorrier for him than for myself, not being able to go sailing on Sunday mornings any more, or tell people about the new central-heating system he was so proud of—we had it installed only last year. You see, it's an old Tudor house, and he had it done, without spoiling the antiqueness. But I can't see myself making a tragedy of it, or of anything that happened to mere me. It's a big world, but made up of little things. Just as history is long, thousands of years long, but one little life ends not far off from where it begins.

ELEANOR: But don't you believe that sometimes really big, really important people are born—people who are something more than insignificant members of the human crowd?

MRS. LYLEY: Of course, there are some wonderful people in the world, and I'm not trying to run down human nature. But somehow I'm always sorry for the wonderful ones—the people with brains. For what does it all come to, but that they're dissatisfied with being what they are, and the world for being what it is? And no amount of brains can change it. They write books that make us laugh or cry over ourselves, but through it all we remain exactly what we have always been. And what's the use of all that intelligence if you can't do anything with it but sit and brood?

ADAM: But some people think that there is something else besides this world—a different sort of existence; and that we're not necessarily doomed to live these helpless, more or less blindfolded lives and then evaporate. Every person who thinks at all is a prophet in some form. Just as when you're young you can't help imagining what your life will be like later on, so people can't help imagining what kind of life will follow this life. It might be thinking a hundred years ahead, or thousands, or beyond that, to when this world gradually comes to an end. And who's to say where the break comes, between thinking about future ages, as a lot of thoughtful people in Nero's day must have prophesied the Fall of Rome to themselves, or thinking about the next world—life after death? And probably a lot of the prophets in the Bible got their dates mixed—when they thought they were talking religion they were only talking future history.

MRS. LYLEY: All I know is that when I'm dead I'll be dead—and perhaps the sign of it is that I don't think. It's better to be sure that you're not going somewhere nice in the evening than to tease yourself all day with the idea that perhaps you will. At least you don't spoil your day. I've enjoyed my life, such as it was, and I'm not spoiling it with thoughts of theatre-going and parties and champagne suppers later on. And as for the prophets in the Bible, they couldn't have been so sure, or they wouldn't have been such gloomy, ill-tempered old cranks and bullies. How did they know that people wanted to go on for ever and ever and ever? Some people—most people, I think—get naturally tired; and it's a wise dog that knows when he's had enough.

ELEANOR: The trouble is, one can't say anything that applies to everybody. No matter how true it may be of some people, it isn't true on the whole—because there are people and people. There's no average person you can generalize about. Everybody's a little eccentric, except people like Number Seventeen here, and me, perhaps—and we're not very real, as people go. The most you could say about us was that we disagreed somewhat with everybody, and didn't agree among ourselves, and that we weren't very happy or very unhappy; and that, while we had a lot of ideas, we had no single very positive idea—well, in a word, that we were neutral. Like Sundays: we're Sunday people. It's the other days of the week that count, really. But, on the other hand, you can't roll them up into one.

ADAM: No, there's Monday, and Tuesday, and then Wednesday, and then of course Thursday, and Friday is also a day, and as for Saturday.... Still, you always come round to Sunday, and that's us. We're everybody's day of rest.

MRS. LYLEY: You can keep your Sunday—all it means to me is a lot of newspapers full of actresses' memories, all expurgated, and no news. And a lunch like a dinner, that weakens your vitality, so that when people come to tea you can't do anything but be polite. And there's nothing that undermines your self-respect like sitting and being polite for an hour and a half. On any other day you'd make jokes—that's what sends up a person's self-respect, feeling you have a sense of humour. But jokes don't come off on Sundays—everybody timid and self-conscious, like at a funeral, and not even a corpse. And then Sunday evenings, of course, there's always an Argument. You sit around and snarl at the dearest people in the world, as if you'd been stranded together on a desert island for years, and were beginning to get on each other's nerves instead of being grateful for their continued company. Where ordinary nights you'd let them talk on, not listening too closely to what they said, just glad to have them around and filling the chairs. I always did have a horror of empty chairs—at any rate in sitting-rooms. That's why I have so few in mine, and all easy-chairs.

ELEANOR: Well, I should say you were a perfect Monday person.

MRS. LYLEY: That's right, Monday for me, especially Monday morning—though the whole day seems like morning. Early in the week, fresh start, clean linen on the beds, all smiles and nothing much happening. Nobody dies on Monday.

ELEANOR: Yes, the people who fret and puzzle and think solemn thoughts all come toward the end of the week. Saturday ones—those are the heavyweights, the ones who'll go on long after all the rest, although life at that stage may be no more than a conference-table in the middle of nowhere, with a squeaking Chinaman at one end and a hammering German at the other, and everybody in between muttering to themselves in all the other foreign languages. Which is why the lightweights take Saturday afternoon off.

ADAM: This kind of talk is like mathematics—you can do what you like with numbers, and add anything to anything else, and the result is a sum. Two and two makes four, you say, and nobody would dare to disagree—except some freak mathematician or whimsical essayist. And seven times one makes seven, and that's seven days, and seven days is a week. But no day's the same to everyone—what's Sunday to some is Wednesday to others. And people aren't the same from one day to the next. You say you can't generalize. But I say you can't particularize. Because everything's a little of this and a little of that. Suppose you have a complete set of books, seven volumes, on—on any subject. Not seven books each exactly like the other, but seven quite different books. Well, you read them and they're not so different after all. Volume V repeats a good deal of Volume III, and Volume VII is really an elaboration of Volume I, and Volume VI merely beats about the bush because it wants to leave something for Volume VII to say, and Volume IV sort of coughs and shifts from one foot to the other and says, 'Now how far have we got, really?'—and as for Volume II, it's made of things they forgot to put in Volume I, or deliberately left out because people might get bored at the start.

And where's the fallacy? The fallacy is that not only can you not generalize and call anything a subject, no matter how comprehensive you think you're making it, but you can't break anything up into numbers or distinct parts or entities, because nothing is distinctly that or this—it's all naturally mixed and muddled, and sharp distinctions are artificial and childish.

ELEANOR: Quite right—life is a general post and everyone is really everyone else. And the answer is nobody. When we all wake up, rubbing our eyes and wondering how much of it was real—presto! there won't be any eyes!

MRS. LYLEY: Now that's exactly what I feel like every morning when I wake up. 'Who in the world is this?' I ask. And you certainly don't seem much of anything, lying there blinking, with no thoughts you can call your own. But it doesn't take long for you to take hold of yourself, and, mind or no mind, get on your feet and be glad you're alive. And no matter how much one person may be a repetition of another, thank God we don't look alike. Nothing gives me greater pleasure than to look in my mirror and say to myself, 'Now that's you, and no mistake.' We all have that much originality.

SEVEN

THERE HAD BEEN a robbery in one of the houses opposite: Nurse Trebble had told them about it early that morning, and Nurse Davis had pointed out the house. It was their eighth morning together, and there were still two more mornings. The idea that a robbery had happened so near was exciting; it seemed to lessen the danger of their becoming boring to each other, and they were both grateful for it, and grateful to each other for it—as lovers at the theatre congratulate themselves on the excellence of the play, their hands tightening in the dark during its highest moments.

The house was a little finer than the others—the only one, in fact, that had not been converted into flats. And two rather smart young people lived in it, and there were two servants, and a younger sister or something who went out with very smart young men, and an aunt or something—at any rate someone slightly dependent but obviously one of the family and there to stay. Eleanor thought that they probably had a shop in Mayfair, but were originally salespeople in some superior stores—where they had met. He was just a little vulgar, and she was just a little too smart, which substantiated Eleanor's theory. For salesmen are never quite so smart as saleswomen, who take pains to seem above their jobs. He, Eleanor decided, was very kind. When they went off to work, which was some time in the middle of the morning, he would hold the door open for a minute or so while she looked into her purse to see if she'd forgotten anything. And sometimes she had; and he would go and fetch it, and there was something so sweet, so lovingly deferential, in the way he handed it to her. The younger sister rarely went out in the morning—probably because she went to bed very late at night. But sometimes a young man would call in the morning. And undoubtedly she would receive him in her bedroom, and undoubtedly the aunt or something didn't like it but was not in a position to make a fuss. Adam thought that they must be young men who hadn't been down from their university very long and hadn't yet found jobs, because they all still looked like gentlemen—not yet Bloomsbury or Chelsea or Advertising or Balkan correspondents. Balkan correspondents had to look very shabby and in order to keep in this condition they came to England less and less, even after they had stopped being correspondents. He knew one, he said, who had given up his job and just lived there on intrigue and dirt—it was always easy to live on nothing, it seemed, where there was a lot of dirt.

The first thing Eleanor said to Adam about the robbery was that robberies were peculiar to certain households; they happened, generally, in households where there was some fundamental carelessness about things—and too much self-confidence. Not carelessness about locks or confidence in things like being one of the winners in a big sweep or succeeding in love or business—but something more universal, something intangible. Thieves, and criminals in general, were wonderful at smelling out weak points in people.

ADAM: Did you ever know a real criminal?
ELEANOR: Only maids who took things, in a fond, humorous way, which is different from stealing. It's difficult for servants, because they're expected to identify themselves with the people they work for, and yet not entirely, so that they never know quite where they are—or who they are. Mostly, when a servant takes things, it's because her compulsion to identify herself with the person she's working for has been in some way suppressed—and appropriating some trivial belonging of her mistress's is one way it comes out, and discussing her mistress's affairs in a possessive way with other servants is another. I think servants must have been happier in older days, when they weren't supposed to lead lives of their own but were really absorbed by the households they served in. And they really loved their mistresses and masters, and they really were loved. A terrible lot of thieving must have gone on in the great houses, but they were more or less expected to help themselves, and honesty was only a matter of degree. Of course, I've known many dishonest

people, but I suppose the difference between a dishonest person and a criminal is that the dishonest person is really injuring himself, while the criminal only injures other people. One doesn't respect the dishonest person, while one does, somehow, have a kind of respect, or at least admiration, for the criminal. One's sorry for the dishonest person, in a way, because he can't help himself; but the criminal seems above pity—what he does he does deliberately, and it's not so much immoral as fascinating. You can't psychoanalyse a criminal, as you can the merely dishonest person. You accept what he does as history, while the dishonest person is more like one of the family—like some relative you're ashamed of. It's this feeling that criminals are perfect strangers, or people living in some other time, that makes it possible for society to punish them so severely, instead of trying to reason with them, as you would with a friend or relative who had done something wrong.

ADAM: All the same, they do have emotions just like ours—sweethearts and wives and families they love and weaknesses for silk underclothing and parties and sometimes even literature.

ELEANOR: Oh, that's just playing at being human. It's only our sentimentality that makes us read into their doings emotions like our own. Just as when we look at a mother cat nursing her kitten and purring over it with private delight, her eyes blinking at us dreamily. 'How human!' we say. Well, it's not human. It'd be truer to say, when we see a mother looking down tenderly at the human kitten at her breast, 'How animal!' And in less than a year the kitten will be sharing her mother's lover with her—probably her own father—and it'll be all spitting and growling between them. But we don't say 'How human!' then. Yet you do have cases of jealousy between mothers and daughters over men, and writers make what is called 'human drama' out of that sort of thing—although, to be quite fair, it's mostly French writers who exploit themes like that. One can't call the French altogether human.

ADAM: It's generally the English who people say aren't human.

ELEANOR: That's because they're human in a proud sense, and in popular terminology 'human being' has come to mean 'poor thing.' The English set themselves certain high standards that it's just possible to keep up to—not too high. But they do conform to their standards. Germans set themselves standards that are, humanly, too high, and so they can't conform to them, and so in the ordinary details of life they have no standards, and so they're just ponderous brutes—though they go about like fallen angels, aggrieved because Nature hasn't endowed them with wings. And of course somebody else is always to blame: they never think of blaming themselves—for being too ambitious. And as for the French, they set themselves the lowest possible standards—standards which are very easy to surpass. Animal standards, really; and the human level is a polite version of the animals. All those human animals in La Fontaine's fables—the French really are like that.

ADAM: But it's pretty difficult, especially in oneself, drawing the line between what's animal and what's human. Especially when you see trained monkeys at work, drinking solemnly out of cups and making little personal movements that have something *so* human about them. My mother used to say, when one of us had done something thoughtless, 'My dear, never forget that there are *always* consequences.' I suppose you could say that animals don't think of the consequences. Which is why sex is an animal thing, no matter how human the people are who do it: they don't think of the consequences. Of course, there are people who do it chiefly in order to have children—or so they say, though I don't believe it. They may know that doing it results in children, but no matter how foreseen the child is, theoretically, as a consequence, actually it's something unforeseen and terribly risky. And *while* they're doing it the chief thing is, how nice it is, and nothing else matters—not even the kind of room, not even the other person, or what other people would say if they knew, in the case of an illegitimate love-affair.

ELEANOR: You seem to know a lot about it.

ADAM: A person may be a virgin, but it doesn't do to speak like a virgin, or think like one. One may never have been to Arabia, but one can know a lot about it all the same and speak intelligently about the Arabs. It isn't as if sex were like some out-of-the-way Polynesian island whose mysteries were known only to one or two field-workers. You might as well say that a man must have lived in ancient Greece in order to be an authority on ancient Greece. In fact, if he had lived in ancient Greece he wouldn't be such a reliable authority, from our point of view, as someone living now who had specialized in ancient Greek history.

ELEANOR: No, I wouldn't say exactly that birds made the best ornithologists, or stamps the best philatelists. But as a matter of pure curiosity, are you a virgin?

ADAM: It all depends on how arbitrary your definition is. One can come awfully near, you know, without actually—

ELEANOR: I didn't ask you to be technical or disgusting.

ADAM: But you asked a very technical question. All right, I'll give you a technical answer. Yes, I'm a virgin. Are you?

ELEANOR: None of your business.

ADAM: But you asked me!

ELEANOR: A man can tell a woman a lot of things, and it's decent—it's a confidence. But if a woman tells a man a lot of things, it's an indiscretion—just as a man can decently show much more of his body than a woman can.

ADAM: Then you don't believe in equality?

ELEANOR: No, I don't. Women oughtn't to cut themselves to man-patterns. Keeping them subordinate was one way of equalizing the difference between men and women; modern equality is another way—trying to turn them into men to prevent all their female faculties from accumulating into some cataclysmic doomsday storm. These so-called rights you condescend to give us are just ingenious little safety-valves by which you hope to ease down the violence of that storm beforehand. But however you behave to us, you can't dismiss or argue away the fact that we spread beyond the limits of your rational world. We are the overflowing unknown quantity, and sooner or later your rational world will break down—you wouldn't say it was perpetual?

ADAM: Can't you see that—as it is, men are just bundles of nerves? You needn't frighten us entirely out of our wits. All we're trying to do is acquire a little self-control and poise, against the awful day when women descend on us, like furies of eternity, and make a Last Supper of our miserable souls. You wouldn't begrudge us a stoical resignation to our fate, would you?

MRS. LYLEY: It may seem a funny thing for a woman to say about her own sex, but no matter how much I like a woman I always feel more at ease with a man, no matter how much I dislike him. A man is—oh, I don't know—so much more *natural*. Of course, I have some very dear women friends, and I discuss the more intimate things with them, and even laugh at my own husband with them. But I never feel at home with them the way I do with my husband, no matter how much I may laugh at him. Now how do you explain that?

ELEANOR: I should say that it's like with fairies. They're always interesting themselves in human affairs, and adopting certain human beings as their special charge, and so they get to feel more at home among human beings than with their own kind—much as they may laugh at them together behind their backs. It's the same with any kind of work you apply yourself to in a concentrated way. You get used to the strain, and less and less able to relax. That's why working-men who use their hands all the time forget how to carry them naturally.

ADAM: But what's all this about fairies? Do you believe in fairies, like a Peter Pan audience? I often used to wonder what would happen if the audience jumped to its feet and shouted 'No!'

MRS. LYLEY: When they throw a question like that at you it's always wisest to say 'Yes.' Because they only mean that they have a story to tell you; and you may as well not miss it. Or when they say, 'Do you believe in God?' All they mean is that they have a story to tell you about God, and you may as well have it as not. I'm always ready to believe anything they want me to. It's like with reading a novel. You have to believe that it's true, while you're reading it, or you don't get any fun out of it. It takes all the variety out of life if you refuse to believe anything except what's under your nose. And it seems so ungrateful. All that imagination at work to please you, and then you just sniff at it and say, 'I don't believe it.'

ELEANOR: Oh, it's easy enough to pretend to believe in something, just as it's only good manners to pretend you take things seriously that other people take seriously. That's how we manage to get along with one another, though fundamentally we all disagree. And yet people only disagree, really, in their points of view about things—in their ideas. They don't deny the existence of the things themselves—if they did, they wouldn't get so far as disagreeing. If there's a word for something, then it exists. Like the word 'God.' The atheist only means that he doesn't agree with the point of view the ordinary believer has about God. He may say that God is the product of fear and superstition; but at the back of his mind there's an idea of God as something that's not the product of fear and superstition—the product of reason, probably. And when he gets enough people to agree with him, then he'll come out in the open and say, 'God is the product of reason.' And he'll believe that his God is the true one because he thinks reason is superior to fear and superstition. The same with fairies. There's a word 'fairies' and so there must be fairies. No rationalistic grown-up person would say she believed in fairies, but this only means that her point of view about fairies is that they are silly creatures and that the people who play about with them are still sillier. Well, butterflies are pretty silly creatures, and very few people would say they *believed* in butterflies. Yet some people get quite excited about them. It's an easy way out, I suppose—you have to have some tastes, just as, no matter how shy you are, there are certain occasions when you have to talk. There really are people who run about ecstatically with nets hunting rare specimens, and glass cases full of butterfly-mummies from all over the world, and learned societies where the discovery of a moth with a new kind of tail would be received with as much awe as if they were announcing the birth of a new Messiah. Perhaps they feel that the next Messiah is going to be a butterfly. At any rate, you can say that people like that really do believe in butterflies. Personally, I dislike them because of their shape. I never liked bows—my mother could never get me to wear a hair-ribbon as child. I hate broad things that go thin in the middle.

MRS. LYLEY: But you can't get along without bows because it would mean more knots, and I suppose there's some reason like that for butterflies, too. I must say I don't fancy those iridescent ash-trays they make out of them—it seems so poor, as if the object was to get an effect rather than to have pretty things. And so many modern styles are like that—all for the effect, like things you only see from a distance. You scarcely ever hear the word 'pretty' any more. People stand at the door of a room and say 'How interesting!' But the real test is if people go inside a room and say, 'How pretty!' I must tell you a story about my married daughter's house—though it's not very kind of me. You know, it had to be all modernistic—black and silver and everything a smooth expanse of whatever colour it was. And naturally the money gave out, because those simple things do cost—I suppose they have to have special machines for making things plain. So Daddy and I said, 'All right, we'll furnish the guest-rooms.' And we did it all in one afternoon, going to a furniture shop with no artistic pretensions, but everything nice and home-like, with all the natural parts you expect beds and chairs to have, and not too cheap, either, and *fairly* modern, though I wouldn't say modernistic—and it makes me feel sort of ashamed, you know, when people go over the house, as if I'd done it on purpose, though it was mostly a question of economy. They say, 'How interesting!' from room to room, standing at the door. But when they come to the guest-rooms they go inside and say, 'What pretty rooms!' And how clever of you to have your guest-rooms unmodernistic!' Which is quite true, because not everybody feels at home in aluminum surroundings.

ADAM: You can't always judge people by the kind of houses they live in—or even the kind of clothes they wear. Most people express themselves in only a limited number of ways, and the rest is all social routine—a game of self-expression, with people playing the cards that happen to be dealt out to them.

ELEANOR: But who invents the games? That's one of the mysteries like who starts certain fashions. Although that isn't such a mystery, because I've started one myself. I once went into a very large, expensive china shop to buy some teacups—I didn't want expensive ones, but sometimes the cheap things in expensive places are lovely. I noticed afterwards that it was Blair's, the most sacred teacup temple in London—one hears about it, but I'd never been there before. Well, I went in, and I *am* rather grand-looking, so they Queened me from department to department, and of course nothing suited me, till we came to the servants' china; and there were the loveliest cream-brown wholesome-looking cups, both buxom and graceful. I insisted on having them in that authoritative way that spells eccentricity rather than poverty—and what do you think? In less than a month my cups were 'studio' cups, and no longer in the servants' department—I know because a friend of mine went to get some. And soon they were copied by other shops—with a flowery wreath, for breakfast use by the sub-modern. And *I* was responsible for all that. I suppose that's how things get started—someone does some trifling new thing and if it's trifling enough other people take it up. It doesn't mean very much to the person who started it, and it means still less to the imitators. In fact, if the cups had represented something very serious, nobody would have taken them up: it's impossible to start something *really* new, something big. The thing people are most afraid of is something new—something that would change their lives. People don't like losing things, even if it means changing them for better things. That's what Communists don't understand. If they could find a way of reconciling communism with kings and queens and riches and good fun and spirituality and all the selfish expensive romantic emotions that make people interesting to themselves.... And I don't see why it should be so difficult, because all it means is adding a lot more money to the money there already is, so that *everybody* can indulge his desires. There certainly are enough things to go round: millions of things are thrown away every year because people haven't the money to buy them. So why not make more money, instead of trying to divide up equally what money there is?—which would still leave a lot of things to throw away. Then it wouldn't be all competition in having things at all, but competition in tastes, which would be much more interesting.

MRS. LYLEY: Yes, but it would all work out the same in the end, because it does take a special talent to own things—it's not everybody who knows how to bear up under riches. Even those American millionaires we think so crude—there's something brave about the way they spend money. Not everybody could do it. Just as you can take thousands of ordinary civilians and make a fighting army out of them, but not more than one in a thousand will take advantage of the war, to make the most of it while it lasts—since he has to go anyway—and be a soldier, in the real dignified sense of the word. Not everybody's a good actor. You can say what you like about Americans, but the difference between an American film and an English film is that American actors know how to let themselves go and enjoy being their parts no matter how awful they are, or degrading. You have to have the appetite for things; and the poor—I mean those who stay poor—don't have much appetite for anything besides food. The so-called poor aren't poor in food. People can always get enough to eat if they have the appetite. In my experience people don't starve simply because God or society denies them food, but from having desires that aren't really natural to them, like wanting to be a famous artist when they can't even draw a bowl of fruit that looks eatable but do unrecognizable 'abstract' things instead, as if they had forgotten what real food looked like—and so they don't get food, because they're too proud to go after it. You hear of starving artists more often than you hear of starving poor people. This may sound brutal, and no one could be more generous than me, and I couldn't eat my dinner in comfort if I felt someone in the village was going without his. But I do believe in having what you have and calling it your own. There has to be some order in life and some feeling of personal responsibility about things. I know I couldn't take much interest in my home if I didn't feel it was my own—even if it was only rented; although thank God we do own ours, down to the centre of the earth, including enough garden to make us feel we don't live in a Garden City.

ADAM: Yes, it's easy enough for Russians to be Communists, because they have absolutely no sense of property, their own or anybody else's. It's just lack of any kind of ambition, and sitting about criticizing people who have ambitions as greedy and ruthless—and there are some quite decent ambitions. I once let my rooms to some Russians for six months when I had to be out of England. And when I took them over again—well, there are some things you can't blame on the cat—and they didn't even have a cat.

EIGHT

Now, MRS. LYLEY was a simple-minded but not small-minded person. Many people are simple-minded because their interests do not extend beyond themselves; and we call this innocence, if they are not very active people, and egotism if they are. And of both kinds we should say that they were small-minded. Not so with Mrs. Lyley. Her interests did extend beyond herself; but as she did not have much confidence in her ability to help other people in their problems, her ideas were not very well organized and not many—the world would never call on her for advice, and if it did her answer would be that *she* had no head for dealing with other people's affairs, having little enough for her own, which she always settled by making herself happy in the little world which fate had assigned to her. She saw life, that is, as a conglomeration of little worlds. And her interest in all the other little worlds besides her own was confined to a desire that the people living in them should be as happy as she was in hers. Her simple-mindedness, which was neither innocent nor egotistical, consisted in this desire that everyone should be happy.

Eleanor and Adam saw themselves as belonging to

the world; she saw them as belonging to a little world of their own. And she began to wish that they would see this, too, and make such a world, and be happy in it. They both had the same placid detachment from other people, which must mean that they were in sympathy with each other; yet they refused to be in sympathy with each other, each from personal pride in being detached. It irritated her that they refused to fall in love. They were both too strong. People ought to admit to some feeling of helplessness in life and be together in that feeling. That was what love was, and what these two needed.

She was not a match-maker, but she had a daughter who went on year after year not marrying, mostly because, having had a very expensive education and being very generous, she took pleasure in dividing herself and her education among a great many different kinds of people. With the result, of course, that she 'liked' everyone but didn't fit in anywhere very intimately. This, Mrs. Lyley felt, was the chief danger of education and intelligence in general. It was the same as when people moved to town from the provinces: they now belonged to the world at large, but to no world in particular. It was very interesting to mix with other people, just as conversation was interesting; but it wasn't life. Life was something little, not big. Life was somewhere apart from all the others—a privacy you shared with someone of the opposite sex. One person of the opposite sex was quite enough to keep you reminded of the rest of the world.

Mrs. Lyley: But do you mean that when you leave here you may never see each other again?

Eleanor: Oh, we may, and we may not. One doesn't plan meetings, just as we didn't plan to come here together and be ill at the same time.

Mrs. Lyley: But don't you believe that when two people are thrown together and find themselves in sympathy they owe it to—well, to each other—not to draw apart again? I mean, it's like finding something nice in the street that doesn't seem to belong to anyone—it'd be sinful to kick it aside and pass on. Like a rose: you'd take it home and put it in water. Or I know I would.

Eleanor: Well, Adam isn't exactly a rose, and I don't think he'd relish being taken home and put in water.

Mrs. Lyley: He's a dear, and you're a dear, though you do your best to hide it from each other in the solemn expression of your ideas—and I wouldn't think of inviting one of you without the other.

Eleanor: You talk about us as if we were twins. We're *very* different people. The only thing we have in common is that solemn way of expressing our ideas—and our ideas aren't so very like, either—and we're not so solemn, either.

Mrs. Lyley: That's exactly what I mean—you're not so solemn as you make out, and you'd never quarrel because you don't take your ideas as seriously as all that. Which is what makes it so nice—your being different:

you'll always have somewhat different ideas, but you'd rather go on discussing your ideas than waste time in tearing each other to pieces over one particular idea. You may never find anyone again who would listen to you in that intelligent and yet easy-going way—and the same for him. And you make a nice picture together—he with that big, fair head and such stubborn blue eyes, and you with that careless brown hair, and such a sweet smile, but such sharp, prim, green eyes, like a young schoolmistress, and he a very bright though slightly difficult pupil. You must forgive my talking about you like this, but I do think you'd make a wonderful pair, and that's not being romantic but from a purely practical point of view. I can see that you're both rather bored with living alone all the time.

ELEANOR: People are always much more bored by other people than by themselves.

MRS. LYLEY: Yes, but it's a different kind of boredom. Suppose you haven't anything to do with yourself, and you go to a film, and the film's boring. Still, it's better to see a boring film than sit at home and think how bored you are. It's better to run the film down than to sit sulking. Seeing the film brings out all your interest in life, and so does living with people, no matter how much fault you find with them. But drawing on yourself always just dries up your faculties.

ELEANOR: All you say may be very true, but the fact remains that Adam and I—well, we're like dead, I mean finished, I mean, we're not *in* life as most people are, but—for example, the way we feel, talking together morning after morning, not doing anything because we're convalescents, is the way we always feel. We're convalescents by temperament, I mean. We're very interested in everything that goes on, and Adam's a very good architect, I imagine, and he's no fool in a general way, and I think a lot and read a lot and travel and take intelligent advantage of not having to work for a living; there must be many people like us, sophisticated and observant—the cream of modern civilization. But we don't seem to be able to get together, because there doesn't seem to be anything to get together about. You have to be very young, or very naïve, to feel that there's still some life left to live.

MRS. LYLEY: Well, I'm not very young, and I'm not so naïve as I may seem, though I know my conversational style wouldn't gain me admission into sophisticated society, supposing I had the time or inclination, which I haven't. But you can't live to my age and manage to keep happy on not too much brains or money, and with people far from perfect, and yourself no lily-white angel, unless you've mastered the rules of the game. Some people may put them more elegantly and make a complicated philosophy out of them, but to my primitive way of reasoning there are just these two simple watchwords: Be grateful for to-day and look forward to to-morrow. Even if my husband died to-day, I'd be grateful that I was there to see him properly buried, and that I wasn't dying with him and that there was still something left in the world—sunshine and good food and a comfortable bed to think it all over in. And I'd look forward to to-morrow because then the sorrow of his death would be already a day old, and I could begin getting adjusted to living without him. And that's what I say to you: you ought to be grateful that, no matter how out of the world you feel, you're in it—here you are talking to me, and nothing could be more real and commonplace than me. And you can't say that you don't believe in to-morrow, so there's at least that much life left to live. It's not fair to other people, to decide that you're through with things. The world hasn't come to an end *yet*, and while it goes on it's everybody's duty to play the game. Otherwise you sit about like death's-heads making everybody feel uncomfortable. If you and he got together and at least pretended to be alive, by having problems of your own, instead of thinking all the time about other people's problems, why, you'd make the people who knew you a lot more comfortable—me, for instance. You can't have problems all by yourself, or make the whole world your problem, unless you mean to be like God, which also means to take on all God's responsibilities; you can only have problems *with* someone. So I'm going to invite you both to come home with me—I haven't been nearly so ill as you, and there's that big house, and three maids, counting the cook's daughter, and my husband'd love it, and you've neither of you a family to look after you properly. But you've got to promise me that you'll fall in love with each other. It'd be immoral not to, because you seem so much like a married couple already, the way you take each other's ways for granted. If you went off now and never saw each other again—and you're both quite capable of doing it, you're so *cold*—it'd be like insulting all the nice warm things in life that other people value—and that's what I call immoral. *He's* ready to fall in love with you any minute you raise your little finger. But you set a standard of being impersonal and indifferent, and it flatters his vanity to keep up to it. I'm talking an awful lot, and I suppose I shouldn't meddle, but the moment I set eyes on you two I knew there was love there, and also an obstruction.

ELEANOR: You're a sweet person—and I'm not going to repay you by laughing you down. I really will think about it seriously. You see, I do like Adam—but you know how it is with nursing-homes or holidays abroad or weekends in the country: people are thrown together, and they think it's fate, and let themselves fall in love....

MRS. LYLEY: But how else do you expect fate to work? Things have to happen somewhere.

ADAM: Had a letter or something?
ELEANOR: Why?
ADAM: You look full of reminiscences.
ELEANOR: I am. I've been thinking about myself. And there's nothing to think about but reminiscences. One's just a mass of reminiscences. Even the things one says—one always has a feeling of having said them before.

The wonder is that one ever did or said anything originally—though certainly one must have, or there wouldn't be anything to remember. Writers must feel like that, thinking of all the books they've written—pinch themselves and say, 'Did I really write all that?' And I suppose when they write something new they do it in a trance, persuading themselves that the book's already written and all they're doing is to copy out the words from the finished product in their heads.

ADAM: But what have you been thinking about yourself? Reviewing the painful past before stepping out into the painful future—which begins to-morrow, presumably?

ELEANOR: I've just explained that I didn't believe in the future. That's the trouble.

ADAM: What's the trouble?

ELEANOR: You.

ADAM: *Me?* How could I possibly be a trouble to you—to your future? Ex-fellow-patients molests ex-fellow-patient with ex-friendship. Is that what's troubling you?

ELEANOR: Don't be unpleasant. I'm serious. I promised Mrs. Lyley I'd be serious. She says you're something in my future. And as I don't believe in the future, I've been racking my memory to see if you were ever anything in the past.

ADAM: Oh, so that's it! Trying to recall that forty-third incarnation when you were a Syrian Queen and I a poor devil from nowhere. And I overcame the fierce but half-witted guard at your palace gates by telling him that I was a soothsayer and that I had been directed in a dream to come to you to advise you to marry the first person you set eyes on on your twenty-first birthday (which was the next day) when you left the palace on your way to the birthday-party which your uncle the grisly Prime Minister was going to give for you—and where, to make your coming-of-age a really important event, you were to be poisoned. But instead, you were to choose this chap on the spot, no matter who he was, and make the marriage-feast take precedence over the birthday-party. For it was an old family custom that if a girl wasn't married before her twenty-first birthday-party her husband was chosen for her. And this was why your uncle was so anxious to have the birthday-party as early in the day as possible and get you out of the way quick, before you could choose any of the princes who had come to the capital decked out in their provincial finery to help you save the throne from the hands of your uncle's degenerate protégé, whom you were to marry in case the poison didn't work or got accidentally given to someone else or you didn't feel thirsty. And I advised you to leave the palace in a litter, with your eyes blindfolded, and to take me along; and I would tell you the right moment to uncover your eyes. And somehow you had faith in me, because I had made myself up to look so dirty and old and pathetic that you couldn't help believing in my perfect disinterestedness. So the next morning off we went—and you should have seen the look on the guard's face when he came to your litter and poked his head through the curtains, to find you were blindfolded. He kept staring at you, and walking along sidewise, and then looking at me in a bewildered, suspicious way. But being so stupid, he didn't dare to trust his own intelligence, and so he just dragged along, waiting for you to uncover your eyes, until I told the litter-coolies to speed up, and he had to fall behind because of the heavy armour he was wearing. Then I quickly doffed my miserable garments, under which was concealed the most beautiful uniform I could find in the palace, where I'd been prowling about all night, principally in the attic where relics of former glory were stored. And after combing my hair and putting on a quaint little gold-lace cap, I gave you the signal. I suppose, in those old-fashioned clothes, I looked like a story-book hero. At any rate, you threw your arms around me gratefully—I don't know whether you were aware of the deception or actually believed I was someone different, but I thought I'd better tell you now, after all these years.

ELEANOR: That's very good of you. It was just that I was trying to puzzle out just now. And what happened then? That's another thing I've been trying to remember. I don't seem to recall our getting married, after all, but you know what memory is.

ADAM: Well, we did and we didn't get married. We went to the temple all right, and there was a mean, hasty ceremony, but the chief ritual in those days was the marriage-feast and a certain set programme of debaucheries without which no one was considered decently married. And when you turned up at your birthday-party with a husband and said that it had to be a marriage-feast before it was a birthday-party, your wicked uncle, just for spite, had the birthday-cake removed, and it was too late to have another made, because it was such a large cake that there was no more flour or sugar or eggs left in the city. Of course, there being no cake made everyone uncomfortable, and we sat about half-heartedly, and the fun just didn't begin. And somehow, although you were now technically married and your uncle had to retire with his protégé a broken and disappointed old man (he turned his palace into an hotel, since he couldn't be Prime Minister any more and yet was used to living on a large scale, and being surrounded by lots of people—and all those rejected provincial suitors used to go there, and naturally many plots were hatched against you, but what with the place getting a bad name because of the protégé's carryings-on with the guests both male and female, and the princes running up large bills they couldn't pay and their fathers wouldn't pay, wanting them to come back home and marry the daughters of petty nobles who were after all the people who owned the land)—well, somehow our marriage didn't materialize; I don't think I ever passed through the palace gates again. Perhaps the half-witted guard killed me when I came back with you. Or perhaps

I got the poisoned wine intended for you. Or perhaps I couldn't bear to part with my beggar's rags and took to the road again at the stroke of midnight—since anyway you began to have an uneasy feeling about me after the first flush of magic had worn off (perhaps you recognized the frogs on your grandfather's tunic that you used to finger as a child when he dandled you on his knee). But here we are, however it was.

ELEANOR: Yes, that's the trouble.

ADAM: There you go again about trouble; I think we're very lucky to have both survived that foolish history, and still have our future before us. And then one day we'll meet and know each other instantly and exchange a look of passionate recognition. Elinor Glyn has a story like that. But they suppress the feeling of having known each other in ages past until they can't stand it any longer and go off into the woods or somewhere else in Nature on an excursion—and the wild life they see stirs the primal emotions in them. Elinor Glyn puts it all into a marvellous phrase. Something like : 'Have you ever heard the stags roaring at the mating-season?' Now have you?

ELEANOR: Perhaps that's what Mrs. Lyley means by inviting us to visit her in the country.

ADAM: Oh, has she?

ELEANOR: Yes. But she says we have to fall in love.

ADAM: When? Before or during or after?

ELEANOR: Well, I was just trying to place it myself. You see, I'd rather like to go to visit her from here, because

I don't feel quite strong enough to go back to my flat. She says that she has enough servants and a large house, and that her husband would be delighted—she won't have me without you or you without me. She doesn't think you ought to go back to a brisk bachelor life yet, either. But she says we have to fall in love. And so I've been trying to remember if we ever have been in love, because I certainly can't see it as anything that will happen if it hasn't already happened.

ADAM: I entirely agree with you. And it would be rather nice to visit her. It's even exciting. It's like a story. It's a truly charming incident, and it takes the realistic edge off being ill. How very, very kind of her—and she scarcely knows us!

ELEANOR: Don't be so superficial and ungrateful. She sincerely means it, in a personal way, and she's sincerely interested in us—in an intelligent way. But we have to fall in love.

ADAM: Then let's tell her we've fallen in love.

ELEANOR: I wouldn't like to deceive her, and I don't think we could deceive her.

ADAM: Oh, but I meant it! After all, it's a question of definition. We can use the word and make up our own definition. And isn't that what most people do? They use the word at the beginning without attaching any definition to it, and then spend the rest of their lives working out their particular definition.

ELEANOR: If you think I'm going to spend the rest

of my life working out a definition of love with you—

ADAM: Oh, we could talk about a lot of other things. We need only discuss love very occasionally, as one discusses any big topic only very occasionally and in the most informal and nonchalant manner. We might never even come to discuss it. There are other ways of reaching an understanding besides talk. What's the use of sex, if not to make talk unnecessary?

ELEANOR: But I like talk, and I'm not sure I'd like sex. In talk you can feel that what you're saying is peculiarly characteristic of you—that no one would discuss whatever subject you're discussing in just that way. But with sex, no matter how different you are from other people, you can be pretty sure that what you're doing is exactly what other people are doing, and have been doing for millions of years, and not only people but animals as well. That's why I never use my vote. I can't bear the thought of saying exactly the same thing that thousands of other people are saying—it seems such a waste of oneself. Even if there were a hundred political parties, there'd still be thousands of people in each party saying exactly the same thing at every election.

ADAM: But you can't expect to be a political party all by yourself, and you can't expect to have sex all to yourself. And anyway, it's not so wholesale as all that, because once you're behind your own house door, whatever you do becomes a peculiarly personal and private thing. You may sit down to the same kind of meal that thousands of other people are eating—but there's a flavour to it all that you couldn't match in any of the other houses. Even a simple omelette made in one house has an entirely different taste from an omelette made in exactly the same way in another house. It's a question of climate. And that's why sex would be interesting, as a test of the strength of one's domestic climate—so that you could see two dogs do what was technically the same thing you did, and yet it'd never occur to you to make a comparison, or even a contrast. Yes, I think it's very important to establish a strong domestic climate, against the insinuations you meet at every turn that you're like everybody else.

ELEANOR: By doing what everybody else does behind locked doors and coming out with an air of triumphant mystery?

ADAM: That's right. Because some time or other you have to face the fact that you have bodies like everybody else. People are bound to treat your individuality as a human fiction, so the only way to defeat them is to do exactly what they're doing—and yet be different.

ELEANOR: And does it necessarily take two to play at that game?

ADAM: It happens to take two with sex—just as, if you want to go to the theatre, you have to have a theatre to go to. You can't prove your difference from other people on yourself. There has to be something like a play, where you're merely one of the audience, but with a world of difference between your reactions and those of the people sitting around you. That's what's so convenient about sex. Every man is really the same play that every woman goes to see, and *vice versa*, but it's all neatly arranged so that you can make a private thing out of public property. Just as you sometimes hear a man referring, in a broad, classical way, to 'the wife'—it may be his, or it may be yours, according to the sense.

ELEANOR: You're not a bad talker for a man, and what you say is very like the sort of thing I'd say myself if I were trying to argue somebody into letting herself fall in love with somebody else—a woman who had roughly the same self-conscious dislike of chance as I have, the same distaste for impulsive behaviour. But presumably she'd have some positive feeling about the somebody else in question, or it wouldn't come to discussing the matter. And however much we might agree about the reasonableness of a potential love-relation between two such careful people as ourselves, I don't think anything so negative would satisfy Mrs. Lyley. Which is why I was thinking, when you came out, whether I had ever had a positive feeling about you. Now, have you ever had a positive feeling about me? Don't grin at me like that. This is really serious—because if we haven't any positive feelings for each other she won't invite us.

ADAM: What I think about it is that we ought to accept her invitation and let things develop. I'm sure she wouldn't object to it on those terms. Personally, I feel too weak yet to say all that I feel ought to be said in the circumstances. And I don't think they ought to be said in dressing-gowns. It'd seem so ephemeral—like breakfast-talk. And then there's Miss Kenwood—wouldn't it be disloyal to her, because she warned us? We might at least, out of consideration for her, just let things develop.

ELEANOR: I think you're the most vulgar person I've ever met. Trying to *tease* me, and when I paid you the compliment of talking to you so openly.

ADAM: Well, it's vulgar to let yourself be teased, and it's vulgar to pay compliments, and it's vulgar to talk openly. And anyway, all men are vulgar in love. What do you expect me to do? Say something ridiculous? Nothing would give me greater pleasure than to say something ridiculous. But you'd only laugh. I've got to wait until I feel sure that, no matter how ridiculous what I had to say was, you wouldn't laugh. And that's what I mean by development.

NINE

MISS KENWOOD KNEW all about it because Mrs. Lyley knew all about it, although Eleanor had said nothing and Adam had only said, 'We want to come and we accept your condition—if you don't mind our being a little cold to each other at first.' Mrs. Lyley felt that she understood Adam perfectly and they exchanged smiles— at Eleanor's expense, it seemed. But Eleanor didn't mind; it was all sufficiently ridiculous, she told herself, to be enjoyable at the moment, no matter what came of it. Fortunately, Miss Kenwood seemed to take Eleanor's view of the situation: that it was all rather artificial, really, and so not worth her disapproval. Nevertheless, she was quite firm that this must be their last day: Mrs. Lyley would not be going home for two more days, but they could not wait for her at the nursing-home. Miss Kenwood did disapprove, almost, of Mrs. Lyley's taking all this responsibility, after having been ill herself; she had gone into the matter with Mr. Lyley the afternoon before. 'I know my wife,' he had said, 'and if a thing pleases her it's good for her. She wouldn't have an idea that wasn't good for her.' The discussion having shifted, from what was and what was not sensible for a person who had been ill to undertake, to whether or not Mr. Lyley knew his own wife, Miss Kenwood wisely decided that there was no real basis of discussion. She had two functions—to look after people, and to get rid of them. There was nothing to prevent her now from a shameless preoccupation with her second function.

'I've arranged with your husband,' she said to Mrs. Lyley, 'that your prospective guests are to stay at the "Queen of Bohemia" near Richmond Park, so that they will be on the Surrey side and therefore easy to collect after he has collected you the day after to-morrow. It's a nice hotel,' she said, turning to Eleanor and Adam. 'We've reserved rooms for you. A taxi will call for you this afternoon at three. Lots of air and very few guests. People go there mostly just to dine and dance, but the music won't hurt you. Nothing like music for reviving strength: it arouses all sorts of exciting petty feelings. The worst effect of illness is the heroic calm it throws people into. They all feel, of course, that they've been at death's door and that no other experience can ever be quite so profound.'

'But I don't feel heroically calm, and I have quite enough petty feelings,' Eleanor said, 'without any music. In fact, I'm feeling rather irritable.'

'Oh, you don't feel really irritable. No woman falls in love if she's feeling irritable. While a man often falls in love with a woman just because she does irritate him.'

'And what makes you think I've fallen in love?' asked Eleanor.

'A knowledge, my dear, of physiognomy,' replied Miss Kenwood. 'I'm not judging from your face, but from *his*. You can always tell from a man's face if someone's in love with him. Every good-looking woman looks as if any number of men were in love with her, but you can't tell anything from it—it's just a beauty secret.'

'Ah, well,' said Mrs. Lyley, 'one only lives once, and one may as well have everything on the menu. You have to pay for it whether you eat it or not.'

'And you prefer indigestion to not getting your money's worth,' said Miss Kenwood, looking at Eleanor and Adam as if she would not have minded their having far more calamitous preferences than that. 'It's like the story about the Jewish father who asks his boy what he would like to have, if he could have anything he wanted. "I would like to have everything," answered little Israel. "What," said his father, "smallpox, too?" "Umph," said little Israel, shrugging his shoulders, "if I had good health it wouldn't matter."'

Adam and Eleanor looked at each other triumphantly. 'A joke!' said Adam. 'At last!'

Miss Kenwood thought that they were, perhaps, being rude. 'Are you being rude?' she asked. 'Had you perhaps decided that I had no sense of humour?'

'Everybody in the world has something of a sense of humour,' Eleanor said. 'It would be a very unfair thing to say of anyone—like saying contemptuously, "He'll be dead one day," as if he didn't know it. We all know it, and that's what a sense of humour is. No, the point was this: we felt that you could tell a lot of jokes if you wanted to—but would you ever tell us one?'

'I always tell patients a joke before they leave. As a sign that I forgive them for all the trouble they've caused.'

'Ought we to tell you one, too?' Adam asked.

'I'm not aware of having caused you any trouble.'

'Why, if it hadn't been for you they'd have been in each other's arms long ago,' said Mrs. Lyley, 'instead of holding back from each other like two nervous boxers.'

'Oh, that,' said Miss Kenwood with a self-congratulatory air. 'I saw that it was inevitable, but I'm a great believer in decorum. As one grows older, it's all that's left to believe in. There isn't a single constructive institution in life that isn't based, fundamentally, on decorum—and nothing but decorum. You can divide everything into what's decorous, and what isn't. This nursing-home, for example, is a perfect little lesson in decorum. Nurses and doctors keeping everything just so—the most indecent things. And how do you cure it? By decorum. The same with love—there's nothing so indecent as love. And how do you cure it? By decorum. Marriage is a nursing-home where love is cured by decorum.'

'Well, I don't know so much about other homes,' said Mrs. Lyley sceptically, 'but I don't call dressing and undressing together and practically no difference between whose body is which very decorous.' She looked to Eleanor for confirmation.

'Yes,' said Eleanor, 'and the feeling it gives you that every married woman has something mannish under her clothes and every married man something womanish. When I was a little girl I used to think that getting married meant that the bride and bridegroom had something done to their navels. Because a dirty little boy once whispered to me, "Married people kiss with their navels." We tried it, but it didn't work, so we decided there must be an operation.'

'I'm going to send Nurse Davis to take you back to your room,' Miss Kenwood said to Mrs. Lyley. 'I don't think it's proper for a respectable married woman to listen to the conversation of an engaged couple.'

ADAM: The funniest thing was Trebble. I wish Mrs. Lyley hadn't talked about it—it makes people so morbid. Trebble simply wouldn't look at me. Blushing away and very bedroom-conscious. I said, 'What's the matter with you this morning, Trebble,' thinking she might have had a bad night. 'Well,' she grinned painfully, 'as you're nearly a married man it makes a single girl feel a little queer.'

ELEANOR: What did she mean by 'it'?

ADAM: Being a single girl, I suppose.

ELEANOR: Poor single girls, poor double girls. Sex is something that really ought to be got over with in childhood, so that one could look forward to a fairly rational adult existence. Childhood is primitive and sex is primitive; it's extraordinary that they haven't been combined.

Children would just adore sex, too. Because none of the things they play at really satisfy them. Poor Trebble. She brought me somebody else's flowers who had too many, saying, 'A bride ought to be surrounded with roses.' And when I laughed and said that I wasn't a bride, she said mournfully, 'Oh, but you're going to be, that's certain.'

ADAM: Davis was nice, wasn't she? 'I've heard things this morning, and I believe them.' And not another word.

ELEANOR: And what will happen to all the people across the street when we've gone?

ADAM: I suppose they'll just get older—like us. New letters in the post-box, and fresh vegetables at the greengrocer's, and all the front steps cleaned every morning, but the people older and older. And then new people, and they get older and older.

ELEANOR: A stop ought to be put to it. I do hope we won't have children.

ADAM: There are ways.

ELEANOR: Yes, I know. But all this birth-control doesn't actually stop it. Because it amounts to people's saying that there are children there wanting to be born, but they won't let them. Which fills the world with ghosts of unborn children, like a Maeterlinck nightmare. What I mean is children really happening any more—not merely being prevented from happening. And do you know—I often think that birth-control is not so much a means of not having children as an expression of the fact that people are gradually producing less and less children. I mean that even if people didn't use birth-control methods, there probably still wouldn't be so many children born as there used to be. It's just a sign; in the same way that primitive women didn't have children except when they wanted them, or when it was appropriate to have them. They hung things around their necks and so on as preventives, but the preventives were only signs to themselves, to remind them that in Nature one thing led to another unless there were specific orders to the contrary. We can't blame Nature if we don't know our own minds. When we leave everything to Nature it can only stumble on from one experiment to the next. That's what Nature is, all experiment and guess-work because we don't give specific orders. But when we do, Nature is ready enough to yield control. The trouble is, we're lazy, and most often it's Nature at the helm, though we flatter ourselves that it's us. So of all the things that happen there are a few of which we can feel that we really meant them to, although our vanity doesn't let us admit it. And with babies more than anything. I had an old friend who died last year—a doctor who was indulgent and modern in every respect except about birth-control. And about that he used to say, 'The best way is not to.' And he was right.

ADAM: Yes, I know. But it seems rather a pity not to use parts of one's body that are there.

ELEANOR: There are a lot of out-of-date things in one's body one doesn't use, like tonsils. I don't mean that

I believe in castration, any more than I think it's wise to have one's tonsils cut out unless they're absolutely incorrigible. Out-of-date things are useful; as history-books are useful. But it would be silly to say that just because there are history-books we ought to do over again all the things people did in them. And sex is really only a memory now. It really isn't more than that.

ADAM: But isn't it nice sometimes to remember?

ELEANOR: Not actually. There's no memory that doesn't make one ashamed, a little.

ADAM: Yes, but what is there to do? Granted that there's nothing new to do, that all the things one can do are old things—still, one has to do something.

ELEANOR: I should think that it would seem a wonderful opportunity to people, after all these thousands of years of doing things, for doing nothing. For having a rest. And staying rested. We're all so tired.

ADAM: Perhaps you'll feel differently when you're a little stronger.

ELEANOR: Don't talk like a leech waiting for its prey to recover from anaemia.

ADAM: All right, but I think we ought to be a *little* more affectionate to each other.

ELEANOR: Why?

ADAM: Well, to help us act our parts better. Just as actors and actresses call one another 'darling' and are rather immoral, in order to keep up an atmosphere of dramatic action offstage. They really are immoral, although it's supposed to be old-fashioned to think about them like that. The only reason people don't think them so immoral any more is that everyone has grown immoral—I mean conventionally speaking, of course.

ELEANOR: What are you trying to say—that we should behave immorally, and that as a first step toward that I should call you 'darling'?

ADAM: Yes, something like that. I mean, let us forget what we think and try to be a little immoral now and then. Actors and actresses must, privately, have lots of ideas of their own, but they throw them aside, and go against them even, in order to be able to perform their job better—which is to behave like *other* people.

ELEANOR: I don't believe actors and actresses have any ideas of their own—that's why they can be so good at their jobs. And I don't want to behave like other people. I don't want to behave. I just want to *be*.

ADAM: Whatever shall we do with ourselves?

ELEANOR: I don't want to do anything with myself or have anything done with me.

ADAM: Then what's the point in our—you know, liking each other and all that?

ELEANOR: Must there be a point to it? Can't two people just like each other—yes, love each other—I don't see why you should be afraid of the word—

ADAM: I'm not afraid of the word. I only thought it might offend you.

ELEANOR: I'm only offended if you mean by it all

sorts of ends and objectives which are really designs on my future. I haven't any future to promise, and I don't ask you to promise me any future of yours. But if you mean by it that you like me without any reservations whatever, then that doesn't offend. On the contrary.

ADAM: I'd make only one reservation: that you have to like me without any reservations.

ELEANOR: That's different, because you're a man. It's impossible to like a man without any reservations, because a man isn't all of a piece one way or the other, as a woman is. A man is a mixture of things, some likable and some not, and the most you can say is that the general effect is tolerable. A woman, for the reason that she's all of a piece, can change as a whole into something likable if she isn't, but if a man isn't likable, he can't change—he can only make the general effect a little more tolerable.

ADAM: Then I have to say that I like you without any reservations whatever, while all you have to say is that the general effect of me is tolerable?

ELEANOR: Who said I had to say that?

ADAM: Well, that's the very least return you could make if I said of you the most that could possibly be said of anyone.

ELEANOR: This isn't supposed to be an exchange of compliments—

ADAM: It doesn't look like it.

ELEANOR: —but a statement of our emotional

reactions to each other. I'm perfectly prepared to say that I have a good reaction to you—quite a good one.

ADAM: And I have a simply superlative reaction to you. Don't you think we'd better hold hands? Someone overhearing us might think we were being ironic.

ELEANOR: I'm perfectly willing to hold hands, but don't you think that would be rather ironic? We're not exactly a pair of blushing lovers.

ADAM: You're blushing like anything.

ELEANOR: So are you.

ADAM: Then let's hold hands.

ELEANOR: I'll take it away if you don't stop looking as if I were saying the most flattering things to you with it.

ADAM: You're not saying anything with it—that's what's so nice.

ELEANOR: Do you mean I talk too much?

ADAM: Now why should you start a quarrel just when we're beginning to go through all the motions like nice doggies?

ELEANOR: Very well. We'll have the quarrel, if the alternative is to go through motions.

ADAM: I'd be sorry for any other man in my position.

ELEANOR: Oh, would you? If it's as painful as all that, why make the effort? No one's asking you to make the effort—except Mrs. Lyley, and only because she thought it came naturally.

ADAM: Oh, it does come naturally—very naturally.

But it would be painful to any other man—he wouldn't understand how much you loved him.

ELEANOR: But I don't love him.

ADAM: No, you love me. You've had lots of conversation with him, but it's me you love. He and you would be eternally stranded in a conversational deadlock. Whereas you and I—

ELEANOR: Have I ever said I loved you?

ADAM: No, but I love you. And I couldn't possibly love you unless you loved me.

ELEANOR: Well, I couldn't possibly love you unless you loved me. So that makes just the conversational deadlock you pride yourself this isn't.

ADAM: Oh, but it isn't a deadlock. If I say I won't go out to-morrow unless it's fine weather, and you say you won't go out to-morrow unless it's fine weather, that's not a conversational deadlock, but an identical expression of an identical hope. And the chances are that the weather will be fine, and that we'll go out together. Or stay indoors together if it's not fine.

ELEANOR: Don't talk so much.